City

wer

Text Publishing Melbourne Australia

textclassics.com.au
textpublishing.com.au

The Text Publishing Company
Swann House
22 William Street
Melbourne Victoria 3000
Australia

First published in the United Kingdom by Cassell 1957
This edition published by The Text Publishing Company 2013

Cover design by WH Chong
Page design by Text
Typeset by Text

Printed in Australia by Griffin Press, an Accredited ISO AS/NZS 14001:2004
Environmental Management System printer

Primary print ISBN: 9781922147042
Ebook ISBN: 9781922148124
Author: Harrower, Elizabeth, 1928- author.
Title: Down in the city / by Elizabeth Harrower; introduced by Delia Falconer.
Series: Text classics.
Dewey Number: A823.3

CONTENTS

Oblivion at the Edges
by Delia Falconer

DOWN in the City is Elizabeth Harrower's debut, first published in 1957. It is easy to see it as a dress rehearsal for her darker, more contained *The Watch Tower*, the final work and acknowledged masterpiece of her four-book oeuvre. But that is to miss the novel's own particular oddness. For all its lightness, it glows with a sense of place and with layers of significance that remain tantalisingly elusive.

Esther Prescott is a Sleeping Beauty. Her mother died when she was small, and her father, for inscrutable reasons of Waspishness and wealth, has kept her hidden from the world. When we first see her she is comfortable in the 'tree-lined citadel' of their Rose Bay mansion but untutored in ambition or feeling. Her older brothers have taken little interest in her. Thus, 'she was shackled from childhood with completest freedom. All guidance was determinedly withheld.'

Only the vulgar Stan Peterson can wake her from this spell, barging up the driveway one night in his 'long, heavily nickelled, American car'. (Those commas are vintage Harrower: precise, almost caressing; crisply and deceptively pleasant.) Stan is a petty racketeer in a postwar city on the make. He is also a woman-hater. But he falls instantly for Esther's calm lustre.

She, in turn, feels aroused by his attention. She would not be the first bourgeois woman to experience aggression as a call to life. For the first time in thirty-three years her hand touches another human being's: 'Thought and sensation, twin fireflies, flew in sparking, agitated circles.' Esther tells him her name, 'and in that moment they were joined.' Within a fortnight they are married.

Like *The Watch Tower*'s evil Felix, Stan is a kind of vampire—although, unlike Felix, he does not set out to destroy another soul. And, unlike *The Watch Tower* which takes place in the bell jar of the Neutral Bay house where Felix traps his wife, Laura, and her sister, Clare, the action of *Down in the City* unfolds in a block of flats in Kings Cross.

The area is not quite the 'bright and wicked' Montmartre of Sydney the prologue promises us: the residents of Romney Court are biding their time before they can afford something better in the suburbs. Already in residence, Stan has upgraded from his ground-floor bachelor flat to a fourth-floor double with a 'green-tiled bathroom...and a balcony enclosed waist-high by a brick wall'.

For a while, Stan tries. He vows to give up his drink, his long-term girlfriend, Vi, and the dodgier aspects of his business. But soon the marriage starts to turn. Stan transgresses, blames Esther, she conciliates; he realises the power of goading her until she cracks, though this risks diminishing the reflected glamour that he basks in. He drinks and rages; they reconcile. The cycle only strengthens Esther's obsessive love. She becomes ingratiating.

Critics concentrate on Harrower's obsessive theme of toxic co-dependence (it is there, too, in *The Long Prospect* and *The Catherine Wheel*) but few tackle her preoccupation with class. Yet here, as in *The Watch Tower*, is a self-made man stripping a woman of privilege until she is his slave. Stan 'wouldn't let a cold wind blow on Esther', and loves to display her in a pretty dress, but can't help chipping away at her tranquil coolness. He is, in the old coin, common.

Within a fortnight Esther is calling him 'pet' and she is his 'Est'. Stan is impulsive and simplistic, with a limited interior life. 'Poor coot's goin' mad!' he blurts as a popular love song plays on the radio. He is fever-ishly envious of Esther's family, and intimidated by them into resentful fury.

As she carried the plates in and set them on the table she said, 'David called in this afternoon. Just to see how I was,' she added when Stan made no comment.

After a long pause he said, 'Oh, *did* he?' and the weight of hostile insinuation in his voice made her freeze. 'Checking up on his low-class brother-in-law, was he?'

'Oh, Stan,' she began hopelessly, and stopped. 'Here is your soup, pet. Come, have it while it's hot. It will make you feel better.'

But the worse crime in Harrower's claustrophobic fictional universe is parental neglect. Failure to imagine a child's wants, indifference to their self, sets up a child for a life of exploitation. Esther is so 'irrevocably' damaged that she can't imagine her life differently; orphanage-raised Stan has no idea how to treat her. They are trapped in a folie à deux. Even so, Harrower indicates that it may be possible for Esther to find a real, if inferior, happiness with Stan—until her coldly controlling brother destroys it.

Down in the City is a novel of close social observation, but other genres crowd around its central drama. Esther and Stan's marriage fails amid trips to nightclubs and seaside pools, and engagements with their up-and-coming neighbours: the Maitlands and their tiny daughter; and the Demsters, a professional golfer, his wife and their teenage niece. Childish Laura

Maitland is a petty tyrant like Stan. She has taken the desperately lonely young Rachel under her wing, but picks relentlessly at her insecurities to keep the girl grateful. Esther, as much as she is able, becomes friends with both women; and, at times, the concentration on clothes, meals and polite conversation drifts into the sparkly territory of Madeleine St John's *The Women in Black*. Nor is the novel above melodrama: Stan's clinches with the tough-talking, nail-painting Vi might have come straight out of a B-grade movie.

Both narratives further erode the Sleeping Beauty fairytale—which the novel seems to lose interest in after a few chapters. Rachel, palmed off on her elderly relatives by an absent father, is a double for Esther, as Laura is for Stan. But, like Clare in *The Watch Tower*, Rachel has reserves of grit that mean she won't wait passively for rescue. By sheer force of will she gets a job, and a boyfriend—a lecturer from Italy, who encourages her to educate herself—and her liberation begins. (Clare is also saved by contact with a young foreigner: Harrower, like St John, suggests that the cosmopolitan 'new Australians' can enliven a city where the shops are closed on Sundays and oysters are eaten out of bottles.) Vi, meanwhile, is a self-made woman: her economic security means Stan can't intimidate her. Only Esther is susceptible.

But what of the novel's thrall to Sydney, whose weather and moods are so overpowering? Why does the writing light up whenever it describes the 'dark, dusty bush' fringing the harbour, a coral tree 'stark and glorious' or the 'strange, pink radiance' of dusk? This other emotional topography, close to the gothic in intensity, creates a second momentum in the novel that may even be more powerful than the monkey grip holding Stan and Esther. Harrower recalls:

> Moving from Scotland to London in 1954, I decided to write novels. I was never homesick for Australia, but after years away I remembered Sydney with great affection and in great detail, and that was what I wanted to write about. I thought of the city in the years from 1945 till 1951, when I sailed away; I was seventeen at the end of the war and twenty-three when I left. The weather, the skies, the stars.

It would be convenient to read this jangle of fairytale, psychological thriller, social comedy and intense evocation of place as symptoms of a young writer's wonder at all the possibilities of fiction. But it is precisely these layers, each brushing uneasily against the other, that give this book its unusual and lasting power.

In the end, *Down in the City* is only so interested in its main storyline. It wants to throw bigger patterns of dark and light. Harrower's almost ecstatically restless prologue tips us off. It begins at the Heads and moves up the harbour to the Cross—only to keep going, eavesdropping on banal conversations, shuttling back and forth between the inner city and the dizzying Pacific, until it watches the 'vast black heavens overawe the earth with incandescent stars'.

It is no coincidence that Stan later finds himself on a cliff at Watsons Bay above the Pacific, that same point of 'hazy infinity' where the novel started; which is also, as a young tough reminds him, Sydney's notorious suicide spot. Stan looks out toward the South Pole and decides to become a better man. Within hours he commits his pettiest betrayal.

For all its bright poise and brilliant light, *Down in the City* is unsettled, flicking constantly between the trivial and the sublime. There is no exit for its characters, except in the oblivion that hovers at its edges. Just as Rachel describes the mood between Esther and Stan as being like high-tension cables ringing above a lonely road, so Harrower's book keeps vibrating long after we close the covers.

Down in the City

PROLOGUE

Along the southern arm of Sydney Harbour lie the
oldest and wealthiest suburbs of the city, beginning
with Watsons Bay on its high narrow cliff, then, strung
in a row along the waterfront and extending back from
it, Vaucluse, Rose Bay, Double Bay and Rushcutters
Bay. Between Rushcutters Bay and the city proper there
is Kings Cross and a slum.

It is three miles and as many worlds from the
peaceful high-walled streets, the tennis courts and
golf course of Rose Bay to the hill of glamour and
fostered disreputability that is Kings Cross. One
holds the white-brick, blue-roofed mansions and
landscaped gardens of the managing directors and
senior partners; the other, the craggy hotels and flats,
the furnished rooms and cement courtyards of the

ambitious and the seekers of anonymity.

Kings Cross is a world of milk bars and jukeboxes, plane trees, coffee shops and cults; a place where delicatessens with names like Muller and Schultz give twenty-four-hour service and stuff their small windows with sausages, olives and gherkins; with sausages, shrimps, cheeses and jars labelled 'Imported', implying superiority, guaranteeing perfection. There, in open shops under the trees, fruiterers called de Sica, Angeli and Strano conjure up cornucopias of pawpaw, passionfruit and pineapple, of loquat, peach, nectarine and fig.

It is a haven for the foreigner and racketeer; a beacon for the long-haired boys, mascaraed women and powdered men. It is Montmartre: it is bright and wicked.

Of necessity, the commuters of the various bay suburbs must pass through the interesting vice of the Cross, and leaving there, skirt squalor on the downhill run into town as they cut alongside the streets of ancient, flat-faced terraces where poverty reigns. But the trams are busy, the traffic is heavy and they see little of either. Only on reaching the familiar city centre do they look round and feel at home.

Here, in this block, a hat shop, a penny amusement arcade, a bank and a cream-tiled hotel stand side by side: the hotel is on the corner. On the upper half of its wall a hectic glass-covered advertisement shows a long-legged girl and a muscular lifesaver smiling at each other past outsize glasses of beer.

4

The dust in the gutter is caught in a hot swirling wind. It lifts, jets fifty yards along the street and drops. It has driven sharp grit into ten eyes and smutted more noses.

A steady hum that rises to a roar each time the doors swing open comes from the hotel—a hum stabbed now and then with a shout and a curse, or a laugh.

A man and his wife sit in their car waiting for the traffic lights to change. A boat in the harbour, a house at Palm Beach, a car for the kids—what next? They wonder.

'How about a trip to the old country? Everyone's going and it makes you look ignorant if you can't say you've seen all those places. You know, London and Paris and so on—all those places.'

'And I could go to Paris for the new season's clothes. Wouldn't that make them green? Just wait till I get back. I'll show them who's the best-dressed woman in Sydney, or it won't be my fault.'

'As long as we're not too showy about it, it might be a good idea.'

Oh, let me be the newest of the new!

The lights change and they are gone.

In the street, propped against the hotel walls, yellow newspaper placards tell, in heavy black type, of a European crisis, a country flood, a murder. The paperboy, his cap on the back of his head, yodels, 'Pi-yup! Pi-yup! Read all about it!'

Trams rattle past and he spits in the gutter. Two bank clerks wait at the stop. They buy papers and turn to the back page.

'What does the *Mystic* tip for Saturday? Little Jonah? Never heard of it, have you? Who's on it? Roderick. Well, there could be something in it. Might risk a quid; what do you reckon?' They ponder, while nearby, three golden debutantes pause for a second to scan the social page.

'Quick! See if they say anything about the party. Paula—you know she's the "Little Bird"—she said she'd get it in for us. Oh yes! She did, too. Listen! "Mr and Mrs Rupert Darley-Banks gave a party last night for their youngest daughter, Miss Arabella Darley-Banks..." Masses of it. Oh, and listen to this! This is one for Rose Breckenworth-Forster! "A certain Miss R...B...F... must like the white lace dress she brought back with her from abroad—we've seen her in it four times!"'

'Good for Paula! Tear it out and put it in your handbag. Throw the rest away. You can't carry an old newspaper in the street.'

On the beaches and cliffs of the coast the breakers crash. The Pacific, white-flecked, stretches out to hazy infinity. The dark, dusty bush waves in the sea breeze. South, the irrigated orchards, long miles of fruit trees, flourish, and in the north, the tropical plantations, the sugar cane. Beyond the mountains to the west great plains of yellow wheat bend and rise acre on acre under a gentle wind, under the deep blue sky, unmarred by hill or cloud, wide as the continent.

In Sydney, six girls from a clothing factory stand on Central Station. They sew tulle, sequin-covered evening dresses from eight till five as an adjunct to their more important task of competing with the American crooners whose records, interspersed with commercials, play all day long. Their ages range from fifteen to twenty. Four of them have full sets of false teeth. Daphne chews a caramel and glances at the train indicator. She opens the evening paper that she buys to take home to her father. Him and his horses!

'Say! Listen to this, Lola. Gloria Delamore— remember, she's that new one we saw at the Galaxy, that singing one in *The Lost Lover*—well, she's married Rock Truton. Gee, she's lucky. It says they're gonna star in a picture together.'

They all listen. Their eyes are shining. One says: 'Hey! Who's goin' dancin' tonight?' They all want to go dancing. 'Me and Al's goin' to the Palais. Hoop-de-doo!'

They catch eyes and start to sing softly, grinning, standing in a circle. On beat, off beat, pause, snap your fingers. And here's the train. About time!

At the entrance to the suburban cricket ground grows a weird grey tree, ghostly grey and leafless; its flowers carve a scarlet arc across the sky. A coral tree, stark and glorious.

7

The surf pounds on the sand at the bottom of the hill, and just along the street the milk bar is crowded, the counter lined with typists, office boys and clerks, who have finished work and want a drink before they go to the pictures, before they go dancing and skating.

The girls behind the counter move with smouldering, sullen speed, their make-up melting with the heat. Stella has four tin beakers in a row. She glares into four pairs of eyes.

'Yes?'

'Chocolate malted. Chocolate malted. Plain strawberry. Caramel malted.' They are meek.

Her face pretends that she has not heard, but her hands work at lightning speed. Half a pint of milk to each beaker, a ladle of flavouring, over to the malt dispenser, a scoop of ice-cream to each, and the first two are under the whirring mixers. She jiggles them impatiently, then, jerking them from the machines, the beaker in one hand thrown high above her head, she tosses a long line of frothing milk into a glass like a cardsharper spreading the pack, and stabs the foam with two straws.

This humidity would get anyone down. Stella has had three jobs already this summer and she won't be in this one much longer. The trouble is they all expect a girl to give up her private life to her work. But not Stella. If Jacko has a day off and says, 'Come on!' she goes. There are other jobs, and she's young this year.

Night comes swiftly. The sun falls with perceptible speed and blackness follows immediately. Away from the city and the glimmer of neon lights the vast black heavens overawe the earth with incandescent stars.

CHAPTER ONE

What was never known for certain was *why* David Prescott acted as he did. Certainly, although it seemed to his sons and his acquaintances a deplorably reactionary, un-Australian attitude to have adopted, it would not have been possible for them to criticise him. And by the time he married again, by the time he persuaded Marion Hervey to marry him, it was too late. As far as Esther was concerned the damage was done, irreparable.

Unwilling, at first, to realise this, Marion, with an urgency that was not entirely disinterested, questioned him on the subject. *She* was not gagged by the blighting tolerance, by the cold ideal that froze spontaneity, which he had passed on to his family. And she wanted affection from David's daughter. She had no thought of playing mother to a girl who had never known a mother, but she hoped at least for warmth and affection.

The boys—David, Hector and Clem—had, with thoughtful responsibility, decided on university, chosen their professions and absolved their watchful father from the necessity of what could only be for him distasteful interference.

They had memories of their mother: they could, and occasionally did, talk with one another, but Esther was alone from the first. She was hovered over, she was observed, but she was not approached. In pursuance of an extraordinary plan which it is only to be supposed was carried out with the intention of securing for her an unusually high degree of self-reliance, she was shackled from childhood with completest freedom. All guidance was determinedly withheld.

It was only when the child reached school age that her father revoked his rule of conduct to make one decision for her. Having succeeded so far with his plan, it was apparently unbearable that by contact with, and inevitably contamination from, the outside world, she should be spoilt. He hired a governess—a Miss Barker, a colourless Englishwoman who spoke well and sewed beautifully.

As far as could be seen by onlookers, this act was the most remarkable of a series which had with reason been called eccentric. If only *now* the term appeared inadequate it was because this was a positive action, the consequences of which might be conjectured: what was past was tenuous, the effect impossible to gauge.

Later, when it was too late, when Marion came, she said what had till then been merely thought by Esther's brothers and her father's friends—that such isolation was unhealthy, even cruel, that she thought, with the best intentions, he had been wrong.

Unperturbed—for when he looked at Esther he was well satisfied by her gentleness and calm—her husband pointed out that the girl was happy. He went so far as to call her in from the garden to ask her, so that she might reassure Marion, and yes, she said, she was quite happy. And, rendered less than happy herself by the expression in the unawakened eyes, Marion turned away, turned back to the piano where she sat, and with one finger slowly tapped a single key until she was alone again with David. She loved him, so she said no more about the past; she simply asked what plans there were for Esther's future.

To signify that this discussion, since it was her will, should certainly continue, that he would answer now but not again, David Prescott went to stand behind his wife, and touched her shoulder lightly.

'We have a good library, my dear, though you have probably noticed that Esther never uses it. We have a pleasant house and garden. Financially she is secure. She has no need of a career. If she decides to choose one for herself, she most certainly has my approval. If she does not, she has it still.'

Marion looked up at him with a gravity that made him smile. 'You, of course, had something more than a career,' he said, referring to the fact that Marion was a musician, had given recitals, 'but I'm afraid we should have known by this time if Esther had had a talent like yours—unfortunately, not. And so,' he finished kindly, 'no more of this—except to say thank you, and I do thank you, Marion, for your concern.'

It was left at that.

Checked, but not deterred, Marion cast about for other means of providing stimuli long lacking from her stepdaughter's life, and very soon the two were regularly attending concerts and plays. They read, shopped, discussed careers and social problems. The first parties for years—and possibly the only parties the old house ever knew—were held at this time. There had never been so much company.

At first some of her brothers' friends were attracted by the enigma of Esther's thin tanned face and light eyes. They were pleasant young men, but polite, and therefore as ill equipped as Marion to penetrate her personality. When they were abashed by her unawareness of them, only her brothers noticed and were disappointed. Even to the girls her unselfconsciousness was daunting, and suspecting that it masked some unnamed superiority, they were correspondingly stiff and unnatural.

Esther moved through these eventful days with willing obedience, for she liked Marion and would have been pleased to oblige her, but, raised in her father's house, enthusiasm was alien to her, real warmth beyond her capacity.

'Did you like that? Were you interested?' Marion would ask, when she had finished a book she had been advised to read.

'Yes,' the girl would say. 'Of course.' And they would look at one another doubtfully, with bafflement, and, on Marion's part, despair.

Quite often her kindness would be met with blank surprise, or perhaps alarm; enough, in any case, to convince the older woman gradually that she was not doing well, that what was done was done, and that she must desist from her efforts. This was, after all, not to be the way that Esther might be led to sudden awareness of life and herself.

The empty days, the months and years that followed this one period of activity, passed with placid, dream-like heaviness for Esther. For hour after hour, summer after summer, she lay alone in the sun in the garden of the old stone house overlooking Rose Bay. This was, in fact, her greatest pleasure—to be hot, to be alone in the sun, to notice the gradual deepening of her tan.

It was only when she grew older that a new interest came, independent of sponsors, to take a high place in the scale of her enjoyments. It was a feeling for the city; a feeling for the tall, light buildings, the narrow streets and crowded pavements; a feeling for the sea and sun in it, the wealth and glamour, the strength and fierceness of it.

The city, to her, meant a few particular blocks—the best blocks—lying together in a neat rectangle, linked by arcades and department stores; three streets one way, cut by four at right angles, bounded at the top by gardens, self-enclosed at the bottom and either end.

Three or four times a week she walked the streets of these blocks, smelt the coffee, the flowers, the rich expensive leather, the cosmetics. She looked through ruby glass in antique shops, and handled heavy satins from abroad. Sometimes when she had looked, she bought—perhaps a print, a piece of china, very often clothes, and she dressed well.

She preferred to be alone, to linger when she chose, to weigh her purchases in silence; but occasionally Marion joined her, and, after he married, Hector's wife, Angela.

Esther was twenty-eight when Hector married, and it was later the same year that her father died. Neither event stirred the deep serenity of the big airy house that was her home. Its furniture gleamed; its vases were filled. On the hottest days its rooms were still cool, and fragrant with garden air.

Incapable of responding to the suddenness of her father's death, though not unfeeling, Esther felt nothing.

15

What her brothers took to be admirable control, Marion more truly interpreted as something for which she was, perhaps, to be pitied, but which nevertheless made her, Marion, turn away in pain and anger.

Soon, however, it seemed that nothing had altered: small changes of routine became established and time went on again. There was a movement of coming together to close the gap. There was even a new feeling of camaraderie, a new lightness, that gave these days an easiness the past had never had.

Remote and unchanging, Esther spent her life in this way until she was thirty-three, when she married Stan Peterson, after having known him for two weeks.

CHAPTER TWO

On a Tuesday night in early summer Esther sat alone by the open French windows in the drawing room. So that she might finish a blouse she was making as a present for Marion, she had persuaded her to take a friend to the ballet in her place, pleading a headache.

Now, while her fingers stitched and her eyes stared at silk, a dozen vague impressions filtered through her mind: the scent of roses, a longing for a cigarette, the look and taste of the lemon soufflé Mrs Ramsay had made for dinner, the line of poplars at the end of the garden. She wondered when David and Clem would be home, noticed that her eyes were stinging a little with strain, and that the room was oppressively quiet. She thought that she must stop to switch on the lights and the wireless. But instead, almost at once, she retreated further into herself, blocked all impressions and continued to sew automatically, unconscious of herself, of time.

Presently, though still in the same trancelike state, she threw down her sewing: it really was too dark to see now. She had gone on too long.

Outside, a sky the pure silvery-blue of approaching moonlight changed as she watched, grew deeper blue, and stars appeared; grew black, and shadows fell across the lawn.

Esther sighed and forced herself to rise: it was with a feeling of stone becoming live that her arms and legs obeyed her, moved across the room, switched on the lights.

A blaring cacophony of mechanical noise burst from the wireless and splintered in the air; it was like being pelted with stones and ice, and was equally conducive to wakefulness. Even as she flew to silence it, Esther was grateful for the effect. For an instant afterwards it was very quiet; no city or suburban noises penetrated this tree-walled citadel: the house was a monument to peace. Then Mrs Ramsay, or the wind, banged a door and it was over. She started back to her sewing.

Halfway across the room she stopped, surprised at the sight of an unfamiliar car swinging up the driveway—a long, heavily nickelled, American car. At the front door, out of range of her vision, it bounced to a stop.

Although this was not a house which encouraged casual visits, the rare uninvited caller usually excited a flurry of interest outweighing the faint disapproval. Now, however, caught alone in the house, Esther frowned with impatience.

There was a slam, a pause, a crunch on the gravel, and then the driver stepped from the path into the room. Esther saw a man of average height, well built, with long straight brown hair and a pale smooth-skinned face. He wore a garish sports jacket, checked trousers, a loud tie.

'This is the Prescotts' place?'

There was a pause, then Esther said, 'Yes.'

'Well, I want you to tell me Jeffries' address. I've lost it. I can't find him. Got to see him.' He gave his order in a voice that made her stare. He repeated, 'Jeffries. I want his address. He works for you, doesn't he?'

Damned women, he fumed; can't understand a simple question.

If it had not been for the brawl with Joe at the Cross Keys, and the fact that he had had more than his quota of drinks for this time of night, he would not have been here. But he was here and he was getting angry. Any of the boys, his pals, would have known how he was feeling, could have guessed how much he had drunk. They would have seen it in his eyes and mouth, in the restless gaze, the derisive curl of his lips, in the key chain rattling furiously in his hand.

19

Esther knew nothing but astonishment at his behaviour, and then at her own, for, after waiting again, deliberately, she said, 'I'll see if we have it. Just a moment.'

Her voice was high and unaccented, but in the rise and fall of tone Stan heard security and superiority, polite indifference to his person and his anger, untouchable confidence, and something else—a kind of fastidiousness—which, added to the other labels called up in his mind, made him look at her as she went over to Marion's desk to search among the books and papers. Until then he had seen her as part of the room, and, being a woman, a strange woman, of less interest to him than the furniture, which, he thought, was probably worth a packet.

He despised all women except Vi, and he knew her so well that she hardly counted. Apart from her, women, as being not male, were dirt, and he did not, as a rule, bother to hide this opinion.

But, hazy with drink as he was, he stared at this one with respect as she bent over the desk. Everything he saw confirmed the startling impression that her voice had made. Rather tall—taller than Vi, anyhow—and thin: not a bit like Vi. Real diamonds on her fingers. As she came towards him, holding out a piece of paper, he studied the impersonal grey eyes, the narrow face. She wasn't beautiful—he couldn't say that—but there was a distinction about her that made him want to stare at her, and at the same time feel that he should look away. The key chain was silent in his hand.

Esther had been conscious of his eyes on her, had supposed him to be still antagonistic, and had found the idea almost, she realised with a shock of puzzlement, pleasurable, interesting. Yet when she turned to him she was startled by the change in his expression. The glum, preoccupied mask had gone; Stan was not constrained by any code of good manners to hide what he felt. He made Esther aware that her heart was beating.

'The address,' she said. 'I'm glad I was able to find it for you.'

Now why had she said that? He was a queer vulgar man. Why was she glad? Thought and sensation, twin fireflies, flew in sparking, agitated circles.

'Thanks. Thanks very much,' Stan mumbled, feeling for his wallet.

They stood face to face while he folded the paper with enormous precision, staring at it until it was pushed into a corner of the stamp section, and then at the wallet until it was restored to his pocket.

'Sorry I barged in on you like this,' he said awkwardly, unused to apologies. 'It was just that I...' He could not think of an excuse, but Esther told him, by a slight inclination of her head, that there was no need.

By this time his aggression had vanished completely, and in its place a conviction grown that, whisky or no whisky, he had found a woman who was the distillation of all those high qualities that alone, in his aspiring imagination, had seemed the unattainable complement to his own extraordinary nature. She was the mysterious, superior one. Now she moved away, and he rubbed a hand across his mouth in bewilderment.

'Well, I hope you find him without any trouble,' Esther said, with the curious lack of emphasis that goes with automatic talk. She hesitated, then added, 'I'm afraid I don't know your name?' It was forced from her, but when it was said she was unrepentant. She must know his name.

'Of course,' Stan said bitterly, 'you wouldn't expect a fellow like me to know enough to tell you that when he comes bursting in, yelling his head off at you. Peterson. Stan Peterson.'

'I assure you—' she began, distracted by the flaring intimacy in his eyes and voice, in her own. She stopped, then said, not looking at him, 'I mustn't keep you any longer.'

'It's all right.' He looked at her extended hand, brown, long-fingered, with lacquered nails, which lay along the side of the sofa. 'I'm in no hurry,' he said, his tone unintentionally smug.

A hot wave of anger rose in her. He had meant to be insulting.

Stan leaned forward and grasped her hand. She sat rigid, more frightened than she had ever been. Someone else's soft human skin was touching hers. The hand that never touched a living thing was clutched in a stranger's human hand. There was a vast singing space in her head: eyes and ears and nose and mouth did not exist. She jerked her hand away and stood up, catching hold of the table to steady herself. The room swayed gently into position; darkness rolled back from the distant pinpoint of light, and she saw pale walls and curtains, deep blue carpet, roses, amber, golden, red. She fixed her eyes on them. Yesterday Marion had looked round the room consideringly, saying, 'We've almost too many roses in here; don't you think so, Esther? Or can you have too many roses? What do you think?' And she had answered...What had she answered? And what did it matter now?

'I think you'd better go,' she said. 'I'm expecting guests at any moment.'

'Yes. All right. I'm going,' he said abruptly, staring at the averted head, the clenched knuckles. He knew if it had not been for the whisky he would never have touched her. 'Just now, it was just...I wasn't trying...' He was appalled and elated by his meekness and his daring, unable to control either. Transparently sincere, he said, 'I wasn't trying anything smart with you.' She looked at him. 'Not with you,' he repeated, and Esther's heart beat fiercely.

The air seemed to stand still around them. The ticking of the small silver clock was loud and slow in the silence.

She gave a short deprecating laugh in an effort to find normality. 'I'm sure Jeffries will be surprised to hear of the amount of trouble you've taken to find him tonight.' She began to move towards the windows, but he stopped her with a question.

'What's your name?'

She paused, inclined to silence for a second, then said, with an air of humouring him, 'Prescott. As you must know, since you found your way here and know that Jeffries is our gardener.'

'No. *Your* name.'

Resentfully she stopped again, looked back at him. They seemed to stare at each other through a wall of water; in every movement of muscle, every tone of voice, they might have been under the sea, isolated, yet linked, slow moving, hollow sounding, strangely coloured.

'Esther,' she said, her eyes held by his, and in that moment they were joined. There could be no doubting the emotion, no honest thought that it might not be shared. Each knew, and knew the other knew, and yet, knowing, could not believe.

'And now, good night.'

'There's more to it than that.'

'I don't know what you mean.'

'You know all right. This isn't finished yet.'

Esther twisted a glittering ring on her finger. Her hands were trembling. 'This is really very tiresome,' she said.

'You've got to give me the chance to talk to you.

24

I've got to see you again,' he urged, and she capitulated: 'Very well.'

'Tomorrow night, at the corner down there? Seven-fifteen?'

'Yes.' She could have screamed at him to make him go, but her voice was flat.

'All right, then; I'll see you there.'

In spite of his success, he felt unsure of himself, without confidence. He found himself wanting to plead, to make her promise, to touch her again, but she stood, tolerating him, looking at him now as if he were the merest stranger, and a tiresome one, as she had said. He was dismissed, and somehow he got himself away from her and into the car.

She heard the engine start up. The long yellow beam of the headlights soaked her and wheeled crazily across the garden before it turned and vanished through the gates. There was just time for her to have moved back from the windows before David's black Jaguar slid to the door. She switched on more lights, and when her brothers came in she was sewing, her hand steady and swift.

Clem and David stood side by side smiling affectionately down at her.

'Hello,' David said. 'Have you had a good day?'

'Idle, but pleasant,' Esther smiled. 'Hairdresser in the morning, that's all. I managed to send Marion off with Frieda, tonight. And you? Have you had dinner? We told Mrs Ramsay you wouldn't be in.'

25

'We had some at George's Bar. We finished earlier than we had expected. One of the directors—Charters—couldn't come, so that holds up the business for another week.'

David took off his heavy glasses, and holding them to the light, found and removed a speck that had been irritating him. He had a lined, scholar's face and a strong-looking body. He was dark, like Esther. Looking older than his forty-three years, he appeared to be what he was—sound, kind, unimaginative.

Clem flapped an evening paper against his leg and said to Esther: 'What would you like to do? What about a film? I haven't put the car away.'

'I don't think so, Clem. I want to finish this if I can.' She held up the creamy material. 'Why don't you two have a game of chess? You haven't played for weeks. I'll get some coffee for you.'

'Good idea! All right with you, David?'

'Yes.' David went upstairs carrying his briefcase.

At the door, Clem stopped and turned back. 'Did I see a Cadillac leaving here as we turned the corner? It looked as if it had come from our direction.' His whole pose expressed the slightness of his concern, the unlikelihood of an affirmative reply.

'Yes.' Esther looked up at him. He was her youngest brother, more light-hearted than either of the others. If she had a favourite it was Clem. 'A man came to get Jeffries' address.'

'Oh? In a Cadillac?' He frowned. 'What kind of man?'

Esther said patiently, 'Just a man. Quite ordinary.'

'It was a queer thing to do, wasn't it? Why did he want to see him?'

'He didn't tell me.'

'Yes, but why come here tonight?'

Esther dropped her hands. 'I really don't know.'

Clem grinned, signalled an apology for his insistence and left the room, already uninterested, remembering the unsatisfactory meeting in the office.

Alone, Esther closed her eyes and took a deep breath. A dozen voices chattered in her brain. She chose to hear one that asked: Why did you lie to him? And she cried, But how did I? What did I say that wasn't true?

For the first time she knew the remorse that comes with concealment where none has existed: remorse that was like firm, bony fingers pressing on a bruise, not entirely painful, pleasing in its pain.

She went about the large, high-ceilinged kitchen opening cupboards blankly, standing, looking, realising dully—cream and sugar; remembering—cups and spoons. The reality of, the necessity for, each concrete object was acknowledged grudgingly by a brain besieged, by senses that surged, phrenetically excited.

She carried through the tray. When David came in a few minutes later he beamed on her, on the shining cups, then, rubbing his hands together, murmured, 'Chess!'

CHAPTER THREE

She stood on the comer at the bottom of the hill and felt the warm breeze blowing in from the sea. It was ten minutes past seven. There was no moon, but a myriad stars, shining white and strong, lit the sky and cast shadows on the earth. Esther raised her face, marvelling at their brilliance. It seemed a night of unusual magnificence.

A few hundred yards in front of her the harbour stretched, dark now, forked and islanded, hung for mile on mile with rocky cliffs and ancient gums, with fresh white houses and limp spring flowers. Ferries, constellations of light, moved across from north to south and south to north, crossing and recrossing from city to suburbs.

She glanced at her watch. Leaving the house had

been too easy, she reflected. All her apprehension for nothing. Clem was out with Erica—quite unexpectedly. Old Mrs Watkins had arrived to see Marion at four and would stay until eleven. And David had brought work home from the office and retired to his study, simply wanting, perhaps, to escape from Mrs Watkins.

Esther had looked in on him for a moment and called, 'I'm going out, David—to the Rialto, I think.' But whether he heard or answered she did not know. She was along the hall and out of the door, running, she thought wryly, like a naughty schoolgirl. As if anyone would, or could, have said: 'Stay!'

She felt suddenly wretched at the memory, and the exultation of a moment before washed away.

Just then the car appeared at her side and Stan jumped out to open the door. When they were moving off towards the city he said, as if he challenged her to contradict him, 'You came.'

'I said I would.' She sat at as great a distance from him as the length of the seat allowed.

Trying to force her at once on to a more intimate plane, he said, 'I thought we might go to a place I know by the harbour where we can talk without—'

He jerked the car to a stop as a tram pulled up beside him, and when he started forward again he did not finish his sentence.

What am I doing here with this man? Esther wondered, not expecting an answer, simply trying to

29

assert to herself her distaste and incredulity at finding herself by his side. He's crude. I don't know anything about him. And that hair oil!

Its scent was overpowering. It made her sick. She hated it and the man who wore it. A complete stranger, and yet he had made her dishonest with her own family. The thought hurt. She was not used to self-criticism, and its necessity shamed her. That her previous honesty had been a negative, untested virtue was an idea she had not considered.

Looking at the familiar kaleidoscope of lighted shop windows, cafés and crowds, Esther tried to project herself, to escape, in spirit and consciousness at least, before he said another word.

And she had actually gazed at the stars! A woman of thirty-three. As if last night's peculiar incident had had some significance—as if she had imagined—as if she were a schoolgirl. Yes, there it was again. School-girlishness characterised her behaviour perfectly.

And you liked his eyes. That's not true. I noticed them, that was all. They had a look—a lost look.

The other voice was silent, mocking. A lost look, indeed.

Esther turned her head instinctively as the words appeared and disappeared in her mind. Her eyes met Stan's for a fraction of time, then they both turned again to the windscreen, to the road ahead where a face hung mirage-like in front of each for an instant, and then dissolved.

Everything had altered. Looking down at the skirt of her dress, feeling the texture of the material under her hands, Esther asked Clem's question.

'Why did you want to see Jeffries?'

She, who never cared, who never asked, whose only queries concerned impersonalities like train times and programmes, had broken her long silence with a question involving people—strangers and their private affairs.

Stan was ready for it. He had expected that she would ask, would have been surprised if she had not.

'I deal in exports and imports,' he explained glibly, 'and Jeffries was going to put me in touch with some pals of his who have some good contacts. He's no spade-pusher, you know. He ought to chuck it again.'

'Oh, I didn't realise...' Esther said, vaguely surprised. 'You have an office in town, I suppose?'

'Not exactly.' He hesitated and then went on firmly, 'I do most of the paperwork in my flat. Deal a lot with people. Live in my car.'

'I see.'

They had crossed the harbour bridge to the north shore and were, by this time, approaching the end of the established suburbs. Stan pressed a brown suede foot on the accelerator and turned the car down a narrow rocky road, badly lit, tree-flanked, ending in a flat dark reserve which had been reclaimed from the harbour years before by an enthusiastic council.

It lay, in the daytime, a dreary brownish expanse, dismal and useless to all except small boys who dreamed of roaming the prairies of the Wild West. But at night, when the bush—an aromatic mixture of scrub and gum, old as the continent—rustled on its perimeter, and the black water lapped against the retaining wall, it had mystery and beauty.

The engine died and they listened to the silence. City, human, mechanical noises were far behind them; no sound but the screeching of the cicadas disturbed the warm air. High-low, high-low, they screeched in chorus, intensifying the silence.

'I thought we'd be able to talk here,' Stan said, and cringed at the sound of his own voice. He smoothed his knuckles over the finger grips of the wheel and half turned to Esther's shadowy profile. 'I said some things last night that need explaining.'

Lightly she said, 'Did you?' and then, with a last frantic struggle against a world of unknown feeling, she went on, 'I didn't notice. But, in any case, it really wasn't necessary to bring me out here to explain whatever it was. I don't know why I said I would come.' She gave a thin, false laugh. 'We seem to be in the middle of the bush.'

Stan felt himself cringe again at her tone. She despised him. Money, and his talent for acquiring it painlessly, easily, gave him a place of respect among his own crowd. Few of the boys were as wealthy as Stan, or as smart. They gave him confidence. He could hardly have managed without their admiration and envy. They made him a big fellow. She couldn't treat him like this—he was a big fellow. Everyone knew he was.

He tried the formula now, as he did when shrill, confident, Oxford-Australian accents rang around him in nightclubs and golf clubs; when their owners looked through him and his party or stared at their too-smart clothes and curled at their voices.

She was one of them. Money meant nothing to her: she was used to it, you could tell. As far as she was concerned, he was just a tramp. Still, she wasn't one of those damned fish-faced types. Last night, for instance, she wasn't all superior, though she had a good right to be, and tonight, when she looked at a man, sometimes you would have said she was thinking he wasn't as bad as all that. That's what you would have said, but Stan wasn't sure…He was afraid to touch her. He, Stan Peterson, of all people, was afraid to touch a dame.

His dumb acceptance of her attitude killed Esther's triumph. This was not what she had wanted.

There was no light but starlight. In the smothering intimacy of the car her awareness of him was agonising. Their dark looming figures filled her mind. They were cramped in a world where there was no light, no land or sea.

Stan spoke her name. She had been waiting, poised, nerves and senses strained almost beyond bearing.

Stan put his hands on her thin shoulders. He was an experienced lover, but he felt awkward now as Esther, silent and rigid, shivered under his hands.

Presently they began to talk in sentences, in single words, in silences. The monotonous creak of the cicadas still occupied the air.

Just after midnight the twenty-two inhabitants of the unfinished road called Harbour View stirred at the, as yet, unfamiliar sound of a car speeding past their bungalows.

Bill Stevens, red-haired, freckled and tanned, sat in one of the toll booths at the city-side of the harbour bridge. He was wondering if Doreen would come dancing tomorrow night, and he shuffled his feet in front of his stool.

The cinemas and theatres had emptied an hour ago or more, and the spate of cars had dwindled; even those who had stopped for supper had gone now, paying their toll, zipping across the tarmac of the broad bridge road.

Gazing into the quietness, he trilled and whistled an old dance tune through his teeth. Then he saw the Cadillac come swerving into his lane, and his eyes narrowed. Driver and one passenger. He tore off and held out the tickets. Stan thrust a ten-shilling note into his hand and his lips came forward in a generous pout. 'It's all yours, mate!' he said, and the car shot forward.

The boy smoothed the crumpled note. 'Gee! First time that's happened. I'm doin' well for myself.'

By the time they had made their plans and said good night it was late. Esther left the car and walked up from the corner, up the quiet black street overhung with trees, knowing that Stan was watching her. She heard her footsteps, saw, ahead, the pale stone of the pillars at the entrance to the drive. She turned to wave again, not knowing if he could see her any longer.

Halfway up the drive she noticed the house, looked at it, and saw that elongated strips of light fell from the windows and lay stretched across the lawn. So they were waiting for her. They would be alarmed. No one knew where she was, and it must be late.

She hesitated for an instant longer, then went into the house, into the room where they all stood, harassed and tired.

Where had she been? David asked. Why hadn't she said? Well, he hadn't heard her. Then where *had* she been, now that they'd all waited up? This was so unlike her.

All right, Clem, he would say he was sorry to Esther. It was true he was hectoring her, being high-handed. He didn't mean to be. He was tired, worried. It was ridiculous, of course: no one wanted or expected to know where she had been. He had insisted that the others should stay up. It was all his fault, and he apologised. Would they all have a drink and go to bed?

But then she was talking, and she said she had been with Stan Peterson. Who was he and what did he do? He was himself, and exports and imports, but that was irrelevant. They would all think she was mistaken, or that they could persuade her to change her mind, but please would they try not to? She was going to be married to him in two weeks' time. She was sorry to have shocked them; sorry to have frightened them first, and now to have told them this.

CHAPTER FOUR

Stan moved from his bachelor flat on the ground floor of Romney Court to a fourth-floor double. It had a kitchen, a green-tiled bathroom, a twin-bedded bedroom, small, all lilac and white, with thin black furniture, a dining and sitting room combined, and a balcony enclosed waist-high by a brick wall.

Mac the janitor, knowing that it would pay well, saw to it that the flat was vacant in time to suit Stan. He was the only one who knew the reason for the move at first, but Mrs Mac soon heard, and after that it was no time till Laura and Bill Maitland and the Demsters knew. They were only slightly less surprised than the Prescotts.

Bob Demster was a professional golfer, and Bill Maitland and Stan played together with him once a week on the course where he was employed.

To Demster, bluff and grizzled, and to the cheerful, up-and-coming Maitland, Stan was a moody character. A queer cove, but a good golfer. Yes, a good golfer, but not, they privately agreed, the kind of fellow you wanted to ask to your home too often.

They were partly persuaded to this view by their wives, to whom Stan was a boor. He ignored them, denied them the small flatteries due from unattached men to married women. What was worse—he seemed not to know that anything was due: debts of politeness to women were outside his comprehension. But more troublesome than his lack of gallantry—which, after all, the men did not dislike as seriously as they allowed their wives to suppose—was his business.

Stan was a man of grunts and nods and silences. If he could avoid an eye or a question, he did, his expression enigmatic. Nevertheless, after a few drinks at the club house he had given enough away—hints of grandiose schemes, not caring how his listeners interpreted them—to indicate that whatever his business might be, it was not legal.

'He's always up to something,' Demster chuckled, half admiring, after a session at the bar. But Bill Maitland from that day kept the relationship strictly confined to the golf course.

'What kind of a creature can she be, do you think?' Laura Maitland asked when she heard. 'She's bound to be a shocking type like him, I suppose, but even so, she has my sympathy. I'll be glad when we can get away from the Cross. I'm tired of having all these odd-bods for neighbours.'

Unlike Esther, Stan had no family to inform. As far as he knew, he had no living relative. And he would not go near the boys. The thought, at this stage, was abhorrent to him, but in any case they were always at the Cross Keys, and Vi was at the Cross Keys.

He circled the idea of Vi, the memory of Vi, very carefully, and standing at a great distance, decided that she would just have to hear it in her own good time—when the news reached her. When she knows, she knows, he thought.

Everything would have to be different from now on, and everyone might as well get used to the new set-up—including Stano. No more drink, no more horses. At least, he amended, not too many. And the boys would have to be neglected a bit, and Vi—altogether.

And then cash money. A matter of looking round till you found some safe little business, he supposed. Put a manager in. An investment, legal as anything. He'd do it like a shot for Est.

Est...God, wouldn't they all look when they saw her. They wouldn't know what to say to her—just as well, too. And there'd better not be any cracks. God, they weren't good enough to rest their eyes on her— rotten, dirty-minded bastards for the most part. Stan chuckled affectionately and then grew sober again. Just let one of them open his trap near her! Just let him try it! What he wouldn't do for her.

All thought led to this thought, and this thought to renewed resolutions and vows. He was startled, even embarrassed, by the strength of his feeling for Esther, and that he alone could know the passion and the will to please that lay under her cool impersonality gave him the most exquisite pleasure he had ever experienced. He was alternately humbled and elated by the realisation that he possessed and was loved by her. And that Esther, who was one of *them*, who could never win anything but respect and homage from the rest of the world, had chosen him, loved him, surely proved something in his favour. That he wasn't just any ordinary bloke, either?

Yet, in the midst of self-congratulation, he would pause with a grimace and tell himself that he wasn't in the same street as her and that was the plain truth— couldn't ever hope to be. She should be treated in ways, too, that he knew nothing about, and he had nothing to guide him but how he felt about her—what seemed fitting for her. And what was? Little enough.

Would she tell him where he went wrong? he asked her one day. He knew he was rough, and he didn't want people feeling sorry for her. Wouldn't she help to put him straight? Keep his manners and his clothes in line with her brothers'?

She protested. She could not bear his suggestion. Please would he not insist? But although he was gratified by her valuation of him and her distaste for the plan, he did insist, and made her agree. If she wouldn't help him, she didn't care about him.

From that moment Stan was in competition with the Prescotts. He went to their tailor and barber; he aimed at their manner, and his instinctive dislike for them increased and hardened. So they would try to show him up, would they? They would try to make him feel small?

Before the wedding Stan had one meeting with David, who tried to discover the nature of his business and to learn a little about his background. But Stan was practised in evasion. Pressed, he had spoken for some time about exports and imports, contacts and American lines.

David had smiled, puzzled. 'I'm afraid I'm still vague about your connection with these things.'

But Stan had made his speech and refused, good-naturedly, to enlarge. 'That's it in a nutshell,' he said. 'There's nothing else to tell. I can give her everything she wants—that's all you need to know, isn't it?'

David implied that it was not quite all, but did not persist. Esther had spoken to him, made him promise that he would not ask for more than Stan was willing to say.

'After all, David, I am thirty-three. Stan is almost

forty. It would really not do for you to question him like a Victorian father.'

David had agreed, with what little resignation he could command, that it would, indeed, be ridiculous. But when the interview was over, conjuring up Stan's pale, weak face, he felt no confidence that he had been wise, and a deep frown creased his forehead. It was true that Esther's money was strictly controlled under the terms of her father's will, and the thought gave him some comfort. He had pointed this out to Stan, but his grin had not wavered. 'So what?' he had said.

'I'm convinced that in his way he really does care for her,' he declared to Clem and Marion later. 'But it's all so extraordinary—so incredible.' He expostulated with them as if, somehow, it were all their fault. 'He isn't what one would have expected. I simply can't understand it. I can hardly believe it, yet.'

'Outsiders never can,' Clem said, lifting the top from his boiled egg.

'Never can what?'

'Understand it. It's probably just as well. If they could, where would we be? Think! Would you pass the salt, please, Marion? Thank you.'

'You seem to think it a matter for amusement,' David said heatedly. 'I'm not so easily amused. I'm really concerned about this.'

Marion moderately said, 'So is Clem—and Hector; so are we all. But we are helpless. We can hope that

Esther will be happy, with him: I do, most sincerely. She's had a very lonely life.'

David, who had been on the way to being pacified, at this last remark let his cup clatter on the saucer. 'Lonely? What on earth do you mean?'

And so, out of Esther's hearing, the talk went on: questions and answers.

CHAPTER FIVE

'The only thing is—no lift,' Stan had warned her when he took her to see the flat. 'But you get used to the stairs, don't you think?'

She climbed, concentrating on the calves of her legs, which were too thin, hoping that the exercise would develop them. She did not regret the four flights. The ceilings were low, the flights shallow, and in the two weeks since her marriage she had, as Stan hoped, had time to get used to the stairs. Second floor and two to go.

The door of flat number eleven stood propped open to catch a current of air. As Esther paused, hand on the banister, a woman passed the open doorway and came back again. She had a pleasant face.

'Good morning!' Her smile was friendly and challenging. 'You're Mrs Peterson, aren't you?'

'Yes, I am.'

'I'm Laura Maitland. I saw you one day from the balcony, when you and Stan were going out. Perhaps he's mentioned that he and Bill, my husband, play golf together fairly regularly?'

'Yes, he has. I've been hoping to meet you.'

They stood smiling at one another. Laura's quick eye was noting the quality and approximate value of Esther's clothes, confirming the impression of Esther's general appearance that had so astonished her in the glimpse she had caught a few days earlier; Esther was chiefly impressed by the strong feeling of warmth that seemed to flow from the other woman.

'Have you got time to come in and see my baby? She's just turned two. I think she's a dream.'

'I'd love to.' Smiling a little at Mrs Maitland's outspoken enthusiasm, thinking how seldom she had ever heard anyone praise her own possessions, and what a surprisingly endearing trait it was, Esther followed her into the flat.

Her appreciation of a manner which, surely, a few weeks before would have seemed at least unfortunate, she accepted as another fact to be noted about the person she had come to be.

Inside, she was formally introduced to a tanned and rosy child whose large grey eyes, fine brows and slender neck, whose air of serious attention, charmed her.

Her mother caught her in a close embrace, fierce

and loving, which Anabel endured, watching Esther over her mother's shoulder until, loosening her hold, Laura said, 'Play with Susie, darling. Sit on the floor and play with Susie.'

Anabel plopped down, her plump brown legs stretched out in front of her, and started to talk to her little Dutch doll.

Half laughing, half defiant, Laura said, 'I'm a proud mother, as you can see.'

'You've every reason,' Esther smiled, liking her, and looked again at Anabel.

Laura Maitland was the same age as Esther, a graceful, full-figured woman with irregular features and strikingly beautiful eyes, blue and peculiarly compelling. Her hair, well cut and softly curled, was fair.

The two women lit cigarettes and leaned back, talking easily until, after a few minutes, Laura threw in the first of her direct compliments on Esther's appearance. Her dress was really perfect, so simple, beautifully cut; and her figure was superb. Each word of praise seemed to burst spontaneously from her lips as if she could not restrain herself a moment longer. Her eyes were alight with sincerity.

Esther experienced a small shock of amazement which soon increased and altered as the barrage continued to fly around her. Her extremely cold reaction had the effect of inspiring Laura to still further compliments, until at last she could have held up her hands for mercy. But when Laura finished with a last heavy volley, speaking intimately of Stan as an old friend, of the difference marriage would make to him; how she had known that Esther, the moment she saw her, was exactly the right person for him, all the distaste, the distrust, began to fall away. Esther felt a need to believe that she was all the things that Laura had claimed for her. She wanted approval—even from a stranger; she wanted to hear that she was right for Stan—even from someone who could not possibly know. And when the words were said, it seemed essential that someone should think her attractive because now, for the first time in her life, it mattered.

A little later, Laura began to speak of her own affairs, taking up the subject of marriage again.

Turning her marvellous eyes on Esther, she spoke of her husband and child with a direct simplicity that demanded respect. Her admissions seemed to be offered as proofs of goodwill, as a surety for her integrity after her precipitate invasion, and Esther accepted them as such, with a kind of mild astonishment. She had a friend.

Drifting to other topics—the advantages of living at Kings Cross, the merits and demerits of Romney Court—they each seemed to detect a kind of complementary compatibility about their points of view.

Finally, after veering to exchange a small amount of family background, Esther said that she must go.

'I'm so glad you've come to live here,' Laura said. 'I've often been lonely. There's no one in the block you can talk to, and all my friends live so far out of town. Of course,' she gave a conspiratorial smile and wrinkled her nose, 'there's always Pauline Demster, but she's older than us, and really...'

Esther said, 'I've heard Stan mention the Demsters. I expect I'll meet them quite soon.' She called goodbye to Anabel, who staggered to her feet and ran to the door to wave.

At home again, Esther wandered from room to room, rearranging the flowers and looking out of the windows. One of Mrs Mac's cleaners came in every day to scrub and polish so that there was little she had to do.

This was the first time she had been alone for a whole morning since the wedding. Stan had received a number of telephone calls the night before.

'It's business, pet—something big, or I wouldn't go,' he had told her after the final prolonged conversation.

His other absences had been short single hours, soon forgotten in their time together. Now she found herself unexpectedly enjoying her solitude because it gave her time to remember.

She was glad that they had not gone away for these weeks to another capital or to the country, or one of the Queensland beaches. It was ideal, and right, that their life should start here and be held together by these walls, that their first memories should not be dispersed, or dimmed by distance. For this reason as well as others, Stan too, he said, had been unwilling to leave town.

So we are both pleased, she thought, and then smiled at the weakness of the word applied to them for any reason.

There had been one unimportant withdrawal between them in all this time. She thought of it as all this time, though it was in fact only two weeks; for a fact of equal truth was that these two weeks had been longer than all the years of her life.

It had happened when they were driving through town a few days earlier on their way to the beach, when Esther, seeing that they were passing her bank, had thought of something she meant to do and asked if Stan would drop her off for a minute.

Stan had neither answered nor stopped; a sullen expression, unfamiliar to her, played over his eyes and mouth.

Sinking back in the seat, she said in a low voice, 'It didn't matter about going today.'

'No place to park, anyhow,' Stan said moodily. He glanced at her reproachfully, feeling that she should have had more sense than to mention banks to him. But seeing the disquiet in her eyes, he said,

'It wasn't that I wanted to stop you, petty, but I just wondered if you should rush in there like that without thinking.'

'Thinking?'

'Well, you know, it might be a good idea if you left an account under your old name. Maybe not in this bank, though—I suppose they know your brothers. I thought you might be going in saying, "My name is Peterson now," and so on.'

'But I was. Why should I not?'

'Might be handy if you didn't, that's all. Please yourself, Est.'

'Don't say, "Please yourself." I only want to do what you think is best.'

He smiled at her then, and was ashamed of himself when he saw the uncertainty of her expression. He put a hand on her knee and said, 'There's a good girl.'

It gave him no pleasure to see that he could shake Esther's assurance. Her pride was his pride, and it should be unassailable.

Later the same day he reverted to the subject of banks for contradictory reasons: to punish himself, and to prove to Esther that she was mistaken if she had imagined he was brusque or evasive. 'Don't believe in them. Don't like them,' he declared. 'Too interested in how you get your cash. You and me'll keep ours where they can't ask questions.'

'Where?'

She smiled because he included her now, but instead of answering, he caught her and kissed her, and they stood afterwards, eyes locked together, their difference forgotten.

Wandering in from the balcony where she had been standing in the sun, Esther heard bumping, kicking noises at the front door and went to open it.

Stan was bent at the knees, leaning backwards under the weight he was carrying. His hat was falling off.

'These flaming stairs,' he groaned. 'Let me pass, pet.' He lurched through to the kitchen, where he dumped the big cardboard carton and other smaller boxes on the floor, and leaned back against the table, breathing heavily. He grinned at Esther and opened his arms. When he was holding her he was suddenly struck. 'Did I say "flaming"? Is that allowed? Does David say it?'

Leaning against him, fixing his tie, Esther gave a smile and said no.

'Then that's that!...Still, when you're carrying a couple of tons up those ruddy stairs...'

Together they stacked the bottled beer from the carton into the refrigerator. Squeezing the other parcels then, Stan strained his memory, gave a few preliminary growling 'ers', and brought out, 'Coffee, fillet steak, mushrooms, butter, biscuits, cheese, ice-cream, cigarettes, chocolates! What d'you think of that?' He was like a triumphant medium.

Esther exclaimed, 'But I'd have done the shopping if I'd known we were staying in. You didn't tell me, Stan.'

He rocked on his thick rubber soles. 'Don't tell you everything!'

The red-and-white curtains flapped out into the kitchen and were sucked back again to the window. The afternoon sunshine had slipped round from the balcony and streamed over the blue-tiled walls. A pile of dirty blue-and-white dishes was stacked on the draining board. In the bottom of the griller the golden fat from the steak had congealed and turned creamy. Liquid ice-cream dripped with ever-increasing slowness from the torn packet into a small pool in the sink. On the balcony, Esther and Stan were lying on padded bamboo chairs.

'Bill's not a bad cove, but I don't like her,' he said.

'She seemed nice.'

'She just gets on my nerves or something, I don't know.' Stan dragged at his cigarette for the last time and ground the butt into a shagreen ashtray. 'Still, pet, if you want to be friends, go ahead. You've got to have some company when I'm out.'

Esther yawned and reflected that three weeks ago someone called Esther Prescott had lived in that big stone house in Rose Bay. When she opened her eyes she could see—and she noticed almost everything she saw with fondness—her feet, Stan's feet, brick wall, blue sky.

Scratching his ear, Stan sat forward in his chair. 'We're on to a good thing today, Est.'

'Oh?'

He pulled his chair closer. 'It's a kind of a tool. Fellow brought me the die this morning from the States.'

'What does it do?'

'Well, it's a bit technical. It's only one of the things we've got going just now, but I think it'll be the best. Now listen, pet,' he said, and paused until she sat up and looked at him, 'I don't want you saying anything about this to anyone. These dies—there's some kind of damned stupid restriction. We just don't want any questions asked.'

'Of course I won't say anything—there's nothing I could say. But—is it really illegal? Could you get into trouble?'

'Me?' Stan prodded himself on the chest with a clenched fist. 'Not likely!'

CHAPTER SIX

Though her heart beat a loud tattoo, Rachel Demster knocked softly on the door of the Maitlands' flat. She pulled at her shorts to straighten them, crossed her fingers behind her back, and waited.

After a minute Laura Maitland opened the door. 'Oh, it's you, dear. Bill's just taken Anabel over to Auntie Barbie's. If it had been left to her, I know she'd much rather have gone down to the park with you.'

Rachel said, 'Oh!' Her eyes clung despairingly to Laura's face.

'Come in and have a glass of iced coffee,' Laura said briskly. 'I'll let you pour it out, and then you can talk to me while I'm clearing up.'

'All right.' An uncertain smile appeared and deepened under the older woman's benevolent eye. Her air of dejection vanished, and she stalked into the kitchen with the air of one completely at home.

'It's in the fridge, Rae. Pour out three glasses, would you, dear? Mrs Peterson is coming in soon.'

In the kitchen Rachel spoke in a low voice. 'I know that Esther is coming down, Mrs Maitland. I know her quite well, too. She thinks I'm old enough to call people by their Christian names, even if you don't.'

She carried the glasses to the other room and then wandered to the bedroom door and leaned against the wall, silent and watching.

'Well, I wonder what's the matter with you today, Rae?' Laura said, finishing her work and looking closely at the girl.

Rachel remained silent.

'You're miserable and unhappy about something,' Laura pursued. 'Come and sit down and tell me what it is.'

The girl stared sulkily at the raised pattern on the wallpaper, ran her forefinger over the swirls and dots.

'Come on!' Laura gave her a little push in the direction of the sitting room.

When the Demsters had moved to Romney Court three years before, Rachel and Laura Maitland had gravitated together instinctively in a matter of days—Rachel with a need, Laura with a need to give.

A brief sketch of Rachel's history, told to her on the stairs by Pauline Demster, was enough to raise

Laura to heights of pitying, indignant enthusiasm for the girl.

Rachel had lived with her childless aunt and uncle from the age of four, when her mother had died and her father gone to work in Hong Kong. He returned on leave every two or three years, but apart from the duration of these short visits Rachel was entirely in their charge. Pauline Demster said that she was a good-hearted little girl, perhaps a bit spoilt and moody sometimes...

Moody? Laura cherished her at once. 'Really, Bill,' she said to her husband at this time, 'they treat that girl, and take as much interest in her, as if she were a canary in a cage. She eats and sleeps, and that's that! It's shocking!'

With the first few words of understanding and interest, Rachel was caught. From that time she belonged to Laura, and all her considerable allegiance was Laura's. After the first weeks of intense sympathy, Laura gave her the place in her life that might have belonged to a younger sister whose guardian she had been appointed, and treated her in the humorous, deprecating way that young dependent things are treated. But she was always willing to listen and talk; she always wanted to understand and advise, and Rachel adored her for it.

'Now, Rae, I can't help you if you won't tell me what's wrong, can I?' Laura concentrated her eyes on the girl's averted face. Her voice was thrilling with reason.

At last Rachel said reluctantly, 'It's nothing in particular. That's the trouble.' She knew that Laura preferred a specific grievance on all but her very best days when she would analyse the indefinable miseries of heart and mind for hour on hour. 'It's nothing,' she said again. 'I just wish I was dead!'

'Oh, darling,' Laura crooned tenderly, laughing a little, 'don't say that.'

Her voice made Rachel cry, as she had known it would, and she watched the weeping girl with a curiously mingled expression of maternal compassion and clinical interest.

'I really mean it,' Rachel said dully, when she had controlled her tears. 'I just don't know what to do.'

'One thing's certain,' Laura said decidedly: 'you shouldn't mope about at home reading these deep books all the time. They're no good to you, Rae. They'd make anyone miserable.' Rachel looked at her sadly, feeling wise, knowing that today Laura saw her as a temperamental child who needed only—yes, here it was.

'Why don't you get someone to go to the pictures with you?'

Rachel blew her nose and silently burned at the suggestion. It was a heavenly day. Company in the sun, company in the air, was what she wanted; conversations like the ones in books, laughter and affection, not Hollywood shadows in a dark, disinfectant-smelling, air-conditioned cinema.

Ah, Mrs Maitland. Laura. Where's your attention today? Not on me. Why don't you read my thoughts and tell me what to do to be happy, to be like you? You're all charm and heart and feeling, and because of that, as rare...more than mortal. Rachel sighed with love.

There was a knock at the door and Laura called, 'Come in!' To Rachel she said, 'It's Esther. Better wash your face and then come back and have your coffee.'

Rachel rushed into the bathroom, long-legged, gawky, feeling better but unsolved. She splashed her face with cold water and dried it. She gazed levelly at herself in the mirror. How dramatic can you get? she asked. And the cold eyes said: Being dramatic, talking out, crying, seeing myself, knowing it, doesn't mean it isn't real. It is.

Laura and Esther looked up when she went back.

'Hello, Rachel,' Esther said gently, and the girl smiled at her, calmed by her unemotional serenity.

Laura offered Esther a cigarette, lit it, and took one herself. They all drank iced coffee from tall frosted glasses and talked about clothes.

When that subject came to an end Laura smiled. 'Rae and I were just talking about happiness when you came in.'

Esther, glancing at Rachel, doubted the wisdom of recalling their conversation, whatever it had been. She looked rather vague and discouraging, but Laura, leaning back in her chair, said, 'Happiness,' again, as if she intended to go on.

In her slow deep voice she said, 'I think the greatest happiness a woman can know is to lie in the arms of the man she loves. I believe I am very lucky. I am happy in every possible way.' Her arms rested voluptuously along the sides of the chair.

To Esther, with Rachel there, her face chalky, this seemed unanswerable. She frowned slightly at Laura to make her stop, but she would not notice.

'Of course,' she went on, with a sudden smile to Rachel, 'I could tell Esther things I wouldn't tell you.' Her manner was mischievous, teasing. Then something made her say, 'But even though you never marry, Rae, you can still have a good life.'

Rachel said goodbye to the vision of her true love and resigned herself to spinsterhood.

Esther screwed her cigarette flat into an ashtray. She was sorry she had come this morning, but since she was here she thought she would try to rescue Rachel as soon as a pause made it possible.

'Take Cassie Roberts—you know, that friend of mine,' Laura was saying. 'She's very contented, though she's never married. She has a good job, and her girl friends, and she goes out with them to the pictures...' Her voice ended on a high, unfinished note, as if many more examples of single happiness were to follow.

Rachel pushed the pile of the carpet backwards

and smoothed it flat again. Her red Roman sandals hung loosely from her thin feet. She half sighed, half hiccupped now and then, holding her white handkerchief pensively pressed to her short upper lip, her eyelids down.

There was a silence and Esther stood up and smoothed her skirt. 'I'm sure Rachel will be all right,' she said temperately. 'I'm going to take her off this minute, if you don't mind, Laura. You'll walk down to the harbour with me, won't you?' She turned to the girl.

Laura ushered them to the door. 'She'd love to. And I have masses to do before Bill comes back. We're going down to the beach as soon as we've had something to eat.' She smiled at Rachel with exasperated affection. 'Cheer up, baby.'

Rachel looked at her and felt the tears begin to rise again. How heavenly Mrs Maitland was! 'Yes,' she said with difficulty, and flew downstairs, followed by Laura's benign laugh.

When Esther came a moment later they walked along the burning, tree-lined street, turned a corner, trailed down a flight of stone steps to the park by the edge of the harbour. There they sank onto the pale grass in the shade of a tree.

'Gosh!' Rachel said, still thinking of Laura.

Esther took off her sunglasses. 'Don't take it to heart, Rachel—what Laura said. Her manner is...she sometimes says more than she means.'

Rachel's heart crawled with indignation at hearing Laura defamed even so slightly. At the same time her spirits rose. She pulled at a shrivelled weed. 'Then wasn't she right?'

'About some things, perhaps. In a way. You'll see how it is yourself before very long.' She was at a loss how to go on. She had felt so little of what Rachel was now experiencing. 'Just try not to worry about the future,' she said; 'everything works out in the end of its own accord.'

'I just have to wait?'

'I think so.'

They sat silent, side by side, Rachel rebellious and unhappy. She scowled when she saw a group of laughing teenage boys and girls walking down the gravel path, through the open space in the wall and along the jetty to the small sailing boats which were moored at the end. They jostled and joked and called to one another in high, ringing voices; they were like some carefree opera chorus or a flock of brilliant, rowdy parrots. Contempt and envy vied for place in Rachel's feelings. She looked away from them to the dark blue harbour. She hated the colour of the water: it was not a colour at all. If she were to scoop a handful up, the watery blueness would remain behind. It was as spurious as life itself—second-rate.

Esther stirred beside her and distracted the savage, living boredom that was eating into her. Rachel admired

Esther, and felt for her none of the touchy suspicion that dwelt with her affection for Laura.

Her thoughts turning from one to the other, she reflected: when Mrs Maitland thinks she knows me right through she'll never bother about me again. I'll be about as interesting to her as a piece of plate glass. To keep her liking me I have to be frank, but complicated, and young and pliable...

She suffered over the hypothesis for a while, then, persuading herself that she had discovered what seemed to be an inherent trend towards self-destruction in the relationship, she decided: it'll kill me.

Liking the dramatic thought, she let injustice stand, enjoying the excruciating hurt to herself involved in any abuse of Mrs Maitland.

She shivered and turned to Esther. 'Would you like to move?'

They drifted slowly across the flat dusty park, the sun dazzling their eyes, heat shimmering in the air around them.

Esther's head ached and she thought of her cool dim bedroom. She would have a shower and then rest until Stan came home. He would not be late, for they were meeting the family for dinner at Cave's at eight.

Rachel scuffled dismally. Suddenly remembering her, Esther's thoughts scattered and she looked guiltily at the girl's pale face.

'I'm sorry I've been such bad company,' she said as they turned in at the entrance to Romney Court. 'Another day we'll go down to the pool together— one day during the week—and you can swim and I'll sunbathe.'

Rachel mumbled her willingness and disbelief.

'But I think you should go this afternoon—even by yourself, dear. It would be much better for you than staying at home. Really.'

Esther tried to catch her eye, but Rachel, letting herself into the apartment, smiled politely in the direction of Esther's chin and said goodbye.

CHAPTER SEVEN

In three months Esther had seen her brothers twice and Marion three times. David and Clem, and then Hector, had called on her unexpectedly on midweek afternoons and found her at home alone; she and Marion had met in town. Stan, however, had not met them since the ceremony. There were always reasons why it was not convenient—business or pleasure. 'I like it best when we're alone...'

Finally David had telephoned to suggest a family dinner party at Cave's on Saturday night. Tonight. And she had agreed, trusting that she would be able to persuade Stan.

He had listened with the sardonic expression that the mention of her brothers always brought to his face, and said, when she had finished: 'The boy from the backblocks goes into café society, huh?'

'Don't speak about yourself like that, Stan. Surely there need be no awkwardness, darling. I wish I could make you believe that they like you because you've made me so happy, and they want to know you better. Isn't that natural?'

'Yes, yes,' he soothed her, preening himself in the warmth of her concern. He felt enormous and powerful as he let her have her way.

Yes, he would go. Yes, he was sure he would just *love* her brothers when he got to know them. Yes, yes, yes.

Esther padded lightly up the stairs, relieved to see that the Maitlands' door was closed. Her head was thumping sickeningly. After what seemed an interminable hunt for her key she had the door open, but on the threshold stopped, surprised to hear the wireless booming, claiming all kinds of excellence for a new brand of self-raising flour.

She walked quickly through the hall and the moment of uneasy suspense turned to delight when she saw Stan.

'Stan! I thought you would be out all day?'

He struggled up from the sofa, but his two companions, red-faced men, remained in their chairs. It was obvious that she was interrupting something.

'The business is done, my dear Esther.' He mouthed the words with elaborate precision.

'Business!' one of the men chortled. 'Haw-haw!'

After frowning at him, Stan turned again to Esther. 'I want you to meet two of my best pals, pet. Nobby and Jock Carter. Known them...' he deliberated. 'Must 'a known these boys twenty years!'

The shiny red faces smirked. One of them said, 'Pleased to meet your little woman, Stano. Pleased to meet her.'

He held out his hand and lumbered towards Esther, but midway across the small carpeted space he lurched and fell into a chair. 'Ah,' he said, and lifting the coloured racing guide that was crumpled in his hand, tried to focus his eyes on it.

Esther's face was stiff. Overflowing from the two small tables were bottles, syphons, glasses and ashtrays. Someone had spilt his drink on the pale rug, and the stain was spreading gradually as the liquid seeped through the fibre.

Nobby said ponderously, 'I don't think she likes us, Stano.'

Jock said, 'God, I feel crook!' He made for the bathroom.

'No, she don't like us. Jock and me'll just clear out.' He drank deeply.

'You'll stay where you are.' Stan glared round the room, his face twisted in anger. He stood himself in front of Esther. 'And you'll be polite to my friends when I tell you. Stan Peterson won't put up with any nonsense like this, you know.' Catching her by the shoulders, he propelled her towards Nobby, and then, as he returned, wet about the eyes, to Jock. Above the wireless, he bellowed, 'Say: "I'm sorry I was so bloody rude to you, Mr Carter."'

'Oh, Stan! Please!'

'Please, Stan,' he mimicked, squeaking. 'Go on! Say it!' His fingers dug into her shoulders.

From the wireless came the announcement: 'We are now taking you over to Randwick to Peter Craddow for news about the starters and riders for the first event of the day.'

Dropping his hands, Stan grabbed his racing guide. Nobby and Jock opened eyes and mouths, fumbled for pencils, gaped.

Esther made her way along the hall to the bedroom, and, closing the door, sat down on the bed, shivering. The shock and humiliation of the past minutes were too close to be clearly understood. She sat, without thought.

After a time she pulled herself round on the bed until she lay with her face pressed to the pillow, her back to the door.

Her eyes regarded the lilac linen threads of the pillow cover, noticed choked-up thicker threads of pale green amongst the lilac. She wondered how and why, and ran a fingernail along a length of green. She closed her eyes tightly.

The door burst open as if it had been attacked with a battering ram.

'Shuttin' the door. Tryin' to keep a man away from his own bloody phone!' In a fury, Stan lifted the receiver.

Esther stared at him. His face was flushed and swollen. His shirtsleeves were pushed up past his elbows; his collar was unbuttoned and the tie pulled loose. His trousers had slipped from his waist and hung swivelled at his hips.

'That you, Lou? Stan here...Well, listen, boy; I want fifty straight on Crabapple...Right you are.'

He tried ineffectually to replace the receiver on the stand, then with a curse dropped it and let it swing by the cord, hitting bed and table.

'Well!' He stood looking down at Esther, his hands tucked in the waistband of his trousers. 'Well!' he said again. His mouth spread in a smile of superiority that struck a vague, premonitory fear in Esther's mind. He seemed immensely pleased with himself.

She looked away, but he continued to stand and leer at her. His expression was smug: his was the face of a tyrant restored to balance by a massacre. He was ready to forgive her. As he savoured her dismay, his smile grew deeper. 'Hm!' he said.

Through the open door, the excited high-pitched drone of the race commentator could be heard from the other room.

'And here comes Jolly Boy on the outside, followed by The Ranger and Lady's Finger. As they round the last turn into the straight Prairie Gal is leading by half a length from Cricket, then comes Crabapple fighting hard for second place—'

As the horses thundered towards the winning post, the voice reported at incredible speed.

'Stan, boy, did you hear that?' Nobby groped his way into the darkened room. 'Cricket won by a length from Crabapple. How were you fixed? Each way?'

'Each way!' Stan abused the horse, and Nobby, for some seconds. His wrath burned out, he finished, clapping an arm around Nobby's neck, 'How about a little drink, pal?'

His friend smiled, his false teeth gleaming whitely in his red face. Just at that moment it came to him that he was in the bedroom, and he saw Esther.

'Ah,' he said, 'and here's the little woman herself, and me not noticing her. And I never shook her by the hand yet.'

Slipping away from Stan's heavy embrace, he made a lunge at Esther, missed, and sliding to the floor, clasped her ankles.

Helpless with disgust, she tried to push him away. 'Stan!' she called. 'Oh, Stan, take him away.' Her voice rose hysterically, succeeded in rousing him from his fuddled trance.

Nobby still clutched Esther's legs, but the sudden descent to the floor had made him feel sick, and he hardly knew where he was.

With a burst of rage Stan flung himself at his friend, and lifting him by his padded shoulders dragged him into the hall, ignoring his protests. He banged the door shut.

A long time afterwards Esther heard the clink of dishes in the kitchen and the sound of running water. She could feel a cool draught from the window on her face.

Rolling over onto her back, she passed her hands over her face: her imagination looked reluctantly to the time when she would have to get up and begin to act and think. Then she was on her feet moving about the room sluggishly, unsteadily, from window to wardrobe to dressing table, purposeless.

I must have a shower. I must do something.

She shivered and knew that she could not make a decision before she knew what Stan was doing. Where he was. How he was.

There was a soft tap at the door, and she turned as he came in, carrying a tray. Not looking at her, he put it on the table and said, 'You'd better have this. We have to leave in an hour.'

'Yes. I know.'

After waiting to see if she would say anything else, he stuffed his hands deep in his pockets and left the room.

CHAPTER EIGHT

Talk sputtered and died when the guitar began to twang softly at the other end of the room. The basement restaurant was shadowy, half empty: the plaintive, melancholy music lingered in its spaces as appropriately as the sound of a pipe on a Greek hillside.

The waiters, members of the race which serves in order to observe the peculiarities of non-waiting man, hovered and leaned with lazy busyness—tall, secret men thinking no earthly thoughts, living no life away from the air-conditioned basements, the Chicken Maryland and the champagne.

A spotlight fell on the guitarist's hands, small and podgy, strumming and plucking a Spanish tune: in the semi-darkness his face was putty-coloured. The thin, metallic scrape of cutlery, the faint smell of food that came from time to time as waiters and trolleys passed his back, revolted him.

The Prescott party peered along the length of the room under the haze of cigarette smoke, listening to the music with false attentiveness, relieved to find a unity in hypocrisy and silence at least.

Hector bore the tedium by pondering on its cause. He recalled the lack of ease that had exhibited itself between the eight people at the table. He knew his own defences and sensed the others'—it was their necessity that troubled him. With an abrupt change of mood he began to wonder why he should expect communication to be easy. Even social communication became unbearably false and difficult if one member of the party refused to stick to the rules. The ritual fell to pieces as soon as there was a failure of effort. They were all made to look as stupid, he thought, as they probably were.

David smoked and drummed his fingers abstractedly on the table, looking under his brows, now at Esther, now at Stan. Their expressions were bland, withdrawn, curiously alike. As he searched his sister's face, he had to believe that she was satisfied with whatever it was she had seen in her husband. She looked at the same time serene and vital. Different. A vague term which hid his reluctant admission that the marriage appeared to be successful—a term he sighed at, a little lonely, a little jealous.

Angela, and Erica, who had come with Clem, held a whispered conversation, raised brows at Esther and Marion, and glided away from the table.

When they had gone, Hector leaned forward and reverted to a theme he had introduced earlier in the evening. 'So you've decided on a holiday?' he asked Stan.

'That's up to Est.' He turned to her. 'What do you think, pet?'

They were all watching her—watching as they had been for hours. 'If you can get away, I'd like it very much.'

'And you can manage that, Stan?' David asked, raising a hand to summon the waiter.

'We'll be on our way by Monday.'

David helped Marion to adjust her wrap and everyone prepared to leave. Angela and Erica came back, smiling, freshly powdered, enigmatic.

They made their way out to the street, chatting amiably, salaamed by the manager. The guitarist was finding a new tune as the doors swung shut behind them. Outside, the air was sea- and tree-scented, relaxing, after the manufactured coolness in Cave's basement. Relieved that the party was over, they guiltily prolonged their farewells.

Stan sauntered round to the car park alone, swinging his key chain and whistling. It took all his determination to whistle with a host of sighs gathered in his chest pressing for release, with his head and stomach unreconciled, in spite of black coffee and cold showers, to the rich and elaborate dinner that had passed in front of him. And worse than nausea, than the sight of three male Prescott faces around him all evening, was remorse. He whistled to keep it at bay as he climbed into the car, whistled shrilly at the corner as he gave way to a line of cars linked together by the strong yellow blaze of their headlights. But all the time, behind the dazzle and his own reedy noise, lay a sense of loss.

He pulled up by the side of the footpath where the others stood, still talking, working themselves up to a state of repentant joviality before they dispersed.

'Well!' He grinned possessively at Esther. 'Are you ready to come home?'

She looked directly at him, and his grin faded.

'No answer!' Clem chaffed to break a silence that lasted a moment too long. 'Take her by force, Stan!'

And so they parted: cool cheeks brushed, hands touched, and Esther waved to the row of faces as the car shot forward up the hill.

Stan said at last: 'Everything went all right, didn't it, Est?'

'Yes,' she answered, in a high voice.

He stopped for a red light. 'It won't ever happen again, Est. Do you hear me?...I won't ever do that to you again.' He glanced at her, and after a minute, demanded: 'Well, what did I *do*?'

Someone in a car behind him hooted; he saw the lights had changed, and moved off again in silence.

Neither of them spoke until they stopped at the garage entrance of Romney Court.

'Aw, hell!' Stan cursed dejectedly, sulky because he had fallen down like this after three months of perfection. 'What d'you think, pet? D'you hate me or something? Mmm?' He was not looking at her.

Not answering, Esther sighed and closed her eyes with weariness, but there was, in her silence, nothing of hate. After a pause she said, 'Let's go up now.'

And if this was not the reconciliation Stan had hoped for, he was aware that her forbearance was more than he deserved.

He went into the flat with an air of angry defiance, directing his attitude not at Esther, but at the possible reminders of his late excess. As he switched on the lights his eyes darted, his head turned, as if he expected to be confronted by his drunken self. Amongst the inanimate, yet knowing, furniture, enclosed by the familiar walls and floor and ceiling, he was ill at ease. Alone with Esther he was miserable, wanting and not wanting to talk to her and touch her.

For all his fears, the flat was quiet and tidy. The wireless was silent, the rugs straight. Esther's newest purchase—a still life of fruit—glowed innocently on the wall. Stan was abashed by the peace around him.

No amount of goodwill could force Esther to break the trance she moved in. She was in a climate, in a country, where some grievous natural calamity had just been enacted, and she was reduced to blankest fear, uncertainty, exhaustion.

Long after she had fallen into a restless sleep Stan lay awake and thought of his childhood, and boyhood, and life before Esther. He remembered the paintless shack way out in the flat brown west; how there was never water, but always dust. Water was the thing, the only thing, he could connect with his mother: she was always saying, 'If we had water...' But then she had died. After that, his father stopped digging and planting and mending fences. He stayed in the house all day, wandering through the shabby rooms, fingering the faded cotton bedspreads, letting the well-polished linoleum dull and cake with dirt.

Six years old, silent, watchful, padding barefoot over the dry, baked earth, Stan would gaze wide-eyed through the crack in the kitchen door at the man with his head on his arms—his father—who scarcely spoke to him now.

Stan could see the small figure trailing around the yard, dragging a big stick behind him, standing on the sagging wire fence and gazing out along the bare dusty road. The sound of a solitary birdcall filled the brown and blue land.

In the darkness his expression hardened; his eyes filled with a brooding hatred as he recalled the day when they came and took him away to the square, red-brick building on the outskirts of Sydney. It was there that he had spent the next nine years of his life. It was there that he first learned that he was a poor kid, an orphan who smelled of the institution. Exactly nobody. The memory of the indignities that he, Stan Peterson, had suffered, made him go rigid, made him glare into the darkness. He thought of the matrons and officials who had controlled their soap-shiny charges, and fed them, but had not liked them, had not even taught them.

How came man on earth? Stan neither knew nor wondered. If he had been asked, he might have said that things were as they had always been. And how was the world governed? He would have found that even easier to answer. By politicians born of other politicians—a great racket, but a closed one.

Once he had known a rule of grammar, a rule of geometry, the dates of some of the English kings, what were the main products of Australia, and when it was discovered.

A fat lot of help that ever was to me, he thought. I just had to make my own chances. A man's used his head and got on, made some cash. He's somebody at last. There hasn't been any trouble yet, either. Better not be, not now that there's Est...

Esther. Why had he acted like that—as if he hated her? He felt that he *had* hated her, too, this afternoon. He had envied her—her life, her family, her very self. He knew it was nothing but the prospect of that damned party that had made him rake up Nobby and Jock and drag them back. That, and the envy and the fear. Sometimes he was frightened of men like the Prescotts.

He was too old to cry. He had not cried when he was a very small boy and he was not going to start now. But tomorrow he would tell her that he would truly die for her—that he would not let a cold wind blow on her if he could help it.

CHAPTER NINE

Rachel Demster hung with her head and arms dangling over the balcony wall, wondering whether or not she would be sorry if she leaned further and fell. She wondered if Laura Maitland would be sorry if she were dead, and she thought not. She wondered about her father, and she thought not. Coming to her aunt and uncle, she saw them now in imagination as she had done so often in fact, as they dripped stickily round some parched, deserted golf course in the middle of summer. They're mad, she thought, just mad! And she sighed.

This must be ennui I feel, she thought, and wondered how to pronounce it. It felt like ennui, or perhaps it felt worse than that. If she had a dictionary she might have looked it up to see if she felt worse than ennui, but probably she would not.

The blood began to pound unpleasantly in her head, so she dragged herself up and flopped back into a chair. Another quiet, hot, horrible, boring Sunday! I can't bear it another second, she thought calmly. I'll go mad. All right—go mad. Who cares? You'd be better off. No, but I'm really desperate, I'll have to do something...And I will. I'll get a job. I'll advertise for one.

Immediately she was appalled at having made the decision, for she knew what she had said, she must do. She had promised herself, sometime around the age of twelve, that she would be truthful and true, just, reasonable and, when desirable, kind to herself; for it was clear that these necessary comforts were not to be depended upon from any other source.

She craned impulsively over the balcony to find someone to talk to, someone to tell, but the cement courtyard wore its blank Sunday look, and the balconies above were empty as far as she could see.

She sat back again in disgust, and tears tried to edge their way into her eyes, but their falseness irritated her. She knew very well that she could bear her ennui—if that was what it was—without tears. It was altogether the wrong time for them.

Head thrown back, eyes fixed on an incredibly high and windswept summer sky, she wished that she could disappear into its cool, airy distances. How much easier it would be than living. How much happier. Imagine floating along like a cloud or a bird, or just being a piece of sunny blue space. Rachel imagined, half smiled, then sighed, and went to find a pencil and paper so that she could draft her advertisement.

'Intelligent girl (17) desires job,' she wrote. She looked at the bald black statement for some time, and pencilled the (17) over and over until she wore a hole in the paper.

If she lived to be sixty-seven she would have to work for fifty years, so it would have to be a good job. But what could anyone do for fifty years?

She rubbed the back of her neck and buried her fist in her cheek, trying to forget that Mrs Maitland had condemned her to remain single and solitary for the same length of time—consequently she could think of nothing else.

But do you care? Is it what you want most? she asked herself nicely. Sometimes it is, she confessed, and pictured a country cottage, roses round the door, babies on the floor, someone simple and kind coming home at night. They would sit by the fire and play the gramophone. And they would never think, and never plan, and never, never change. The country would be fresh and cool: there would be flowers, and a mountain and a stream. She sighed wholeheartedly.

Her aunt had always believed that a good and handsome young man would ride up on the allotted day and claim her as his own: a fairytale so often told that Rachel herself had half inclined to believe it.

Then she saw that, to her aunt, the whole of life was a matter of hoping for luck and happy endings, of holding tight to the catchphrases that promised a golden future. But Laura, Mrs Maitland, was not like that, and she had said, speaking as if she *knew*, Rachel stressed to herself: 'Even if you don't marry...' Obviously meaning: 'You won't!'

And neither, thought the girl, would that other dream come true; that vaguer, more insistent dream of a Rachel who studied and understood, who instructed in the arts of honesty and justice, who ended wars and righted wrongs. But if at least, if only, there was someone who could see, who would talk...

She flew to the long mirror in her bedroom to see if her reflection had any answer to offer, but it gazed back, knowing itself ineffectual, no help at all. Still the same long arms and legs, the same hank of brown hair, and in the eyes, the old look of calm and resignation.

'Oh, murder!' she exclaimed aloud. 'That intelligent girl had better find a job soon.'

In the courtyard the Petersons' car horn sounded its mellow notes, proclaiming an arrival or a departure. Rachel ran out to the balcony and hurled herself half over the edge again, sick for the sight of someone, something. But when Stan, looking from the car window, saw her and called a greeting she drew back, suddenly shy.

Looking higher up, to the fourth space in the wall where Esther waited in the sun, smiling at him, Stan blew a kiss. Rachel's face was solemn with exaggerated shame as she moved further back: she felt that she had intruded unforgivably. So they really did love each other! She was full of awe.

The car seemed to be leaving; she thought she heard it on the road. Creeping lightly back to the edge, she made sure. Yes, it was gone. She shivered as the heat from the warm brick penetrated her arms. Blowing kisses! What romantic lives people lived! So much love everywhere, but no one even to care if she lived or died.

It wasn't fair: but even as she thought so, her mouth curved and her eyes softened to think that anyone should blow kisses to anyone.

'Rachel! Rachel!' Esther called from above. 'Could you come up for a little while?'

'Me? Sure!' Eyes sparkling, she raced upstairs times two, and sometimes three, at a time. 'Oh, sure!' Rachel Demster would always oblige and be where she was wanted. Just call and she would come.

Upstairs, she found Esther very friendly, very welcoming. 'What's happening?' she asked, waving a hand at the confusion in the bedroom. 'Are you going away?'

'Yes, tomorrow. Somewhere up north. You'll help me decide what to take, won't you? Have a chocolate?'

Esther leaned forward holding a large box and waited while Rachel chose one. She chewed it appreciatively, legitimately silent, and gazed. She knew that

Esther had no need of advice. Apparently, amazingly, for no reason, she had wanted her company: this was a fact to be thoroughly analysed later, at leisure.

Now, however, on Stan's bed under the window, Rachel lay passive and indolent, active only in one republic of her mind that watched and noted with the cool sharp tick-tick of a machine.

Dragging bright cotton skirts, tops and swimsuits from the wardrobe and drawers, Esther tried to lead the talk around to Stan. She felt that she had, after this morning, reached a new understanding of him, and she wanted someone else to appreciate him, to know all that he had overcome, and all that he tried to be. And she wanted someone to know how far he succeeded. She wanted to say words that would draw a friendly comment—anything kind—so that she could go on.

She would say: 'If you only knew...He told me things this morning, about himself, that—I want to make it up to him so that yesterday can never happen again. And yet, he couldn't help it. If you'd seen him this morning...But, in a way, I believe that as long as he loved me, just me, I could bear it if I had to. The only thing I couldn't endure—' The mental conversation ended.

Instead of saying what was in her mind, she chattered on about nothing, in a shrill voice that Rachel marked as a noteworthy symptom of something—she balked at guessing just what. But apart from its scientific

84

value as a symptom, this unaccustomed vivacity from one whom she had considered the epitome of gentle restraint jarred her sense of what was fitting. Behind her serious young eyes she looked coldly on the animated face and hands.

And then, as she gazed intently into the shadowed eyes, and listened to the nervous, jerky voice, Rachel experienced a sensation of profound pity—for the unknown cause of Esther's uneven spirits, for Esther's falseness to herself, for the fact that she was being studied where she expected uncritical friendliness.

Rachel despised herself. In a frenzy of repentance she fell into an attitude of innocent attention, gradually, with an effort of will, cutting off the machine, silencing it.

Esther was speaking about her family, a thing she rarely did. She talked about her father; she told Rachel how Hector had saved a girl from drowning when he was on holiday on one of the islands near the Great Barrier Reef, and later had married her. She was pleased, suddenly, to be able to mention her brothers' names without apprehension, and found in the speaking a fresh affection for them and for Rachel.

She broke off, lifting a sundress of printed blue and green on white. 'Rachel, you would look sweet in this, and I've never worn it. Do take it, pet. Try it on now. Pauline won't mind, will she?'

While Rachel struggled painfully to undress and

dress without exposing an inch of bare skin, Esther was silent. She had gone back along the path to look again, detachedly, at a thought she had fled from earlier. Stan and another woman. She gave a sudden, pained frown, which Rachel saw, cut short a sigh, and rebuked herself. She knew that twenty-four hours ago she would not have had such a thought, idle as it was.

'I was right. It really suits you very well. You must have it.'

And again her volatile happiness rose to the surface, full of optimism, expressing itself in her restless eyes and hands, in the high girlish laugh, the flow of trivialities.

Rachel, aware in her own nerves of the tension in Esther's, felt another wave of pity, so that she wanted to stretch out a hand and say, 'Don't be like this, Esther. Don't let me be sorry for you, please.'

By this time the floor was a white sea of tissue paper and Esther's bed was a rainbowed barque of satins and cottons. As sandals and bathing costumes began to find their way into suitcases, Rachel breathed occasionally, 'Oh, you're so lucky, Esther!' And, 'Oh!' she would say again, as if no more coherent exclamation could express her envy.

Esther was grateful and indulgent: she wanted to be lucky. She was fond of Rachel, though not with a feeling of any strength, for, having tapped the source of her affections so seldom, emotion of any kind was slow to come; but the girl's admiration pleased her.

When the packing was completed they sat back for a moment in silence, and Rachel was overcome by a spasm of shyness. Esther was looking at her with kindness and sympathy.

'Oh, I'm advertising for a job, Esther—my first,' she cried, swinging her legs for something to do. 'Don't you think it's a good idea?'

Esther said she thought it was. She supposed it must be, since most people were unanimous on the subject. Idly, waving a cloud of cigarette smoke away with one hand, she asked for more details, but Rachel was deliberately vague. In certain moods she would not speak about herself except after the most supplicating encouragement: without it she would on an instant decide mulishly to be offended. Laura had humoured her in this, but Esther did not know the game and would not have played if she had.

Her faint interest faded against the girl's silence, and Rachel, looking speculatively at her from under her lashes, saw that this was so. Yet, recognising her defeat, she saw it also as a victory for common sense, and was wryly consoled that Esther had not plumbed her childishness.

In the courtyard the car horn played again, heralding Stan's return, and the two started, electrified. Rachel jumped to her feet. 'I'm going!' she cried, as if she were afraid of being thrown out.

'All right,' Esther calmed her, smiling. 'But I've enjoyed this morning. I'm glad you came up.'

As they stood at the open front door Rachel paused, and, clutching her new dress close, knowing that she had failed ludicrously in the choice of time, said rapidly, 'Oh Esther, you don't think these are the happiest years of my life, do you? I mean—I'm just going—but, just because I'm seventeen, do they have to be the best?'

Esther had been anxious for her to be gone before Stan came in, but when she heard the question, saw the palpitating earnestness in Rachel's face, she controlled her impatience.

'They *can* be happy years,' she said, 'and I wish they were for you. But judging by my own life, I shouldn't say the best.'

CHAPTER TEN

Autumn came in slyly, in the way of all Australian seasons, with a blustery day here and there squeezed in between late summer scorchers, praised for coolness, not recognised, so far away was last autumn, for what it was: gay striped blue days when freshly washed sheets flapped and cracked in suburban backyards, while along miles of foreshore dark green gums tossed and writhed in the sunny wind.

Ferries shuttling busily between the northern shore of Manly and the city quay suddenly began to plunge deeply, passing the 'heads'—the high stone cliffs which form the entrance to the harbour—as the breakers from the Pacific swirled angrily in the confined space. Regular travellers thought: 'Uh-uh! Winter!' and rolled themselves obligingly to the right and then to the left as the sturdy boats dipped for ten minutes among the waves. They said reassuringly to newcomers: 'Clyde-built! They came out from Scotland under their own steam!' And feeling sceptical but relieved, the nervous ones thanked heaven that they had not made the crossing from the old country.

For some they were dangerous days. Even clever women were known to lose their reputations by blundering into town in white shoes, or by some similar crass action proving lack of sensitive divining faculties, proving inherent flaws in character. But for the more flexible, life was exciting, adventure just around the corner: they were filled with a yearning excitement for they knew not what. Scudding snowball clouds jumped across the blue; the air was crisp and conversation witty; appetites long satisfied by fruit and lettuce demanded more sustaining food. But when the tomorrows came, it was hot and dusty and dry again, and the yesterdays were quite forgotten.

Finally, when it seemed that summer would never end, that glare and humidity were eternal, winter came in with a bitter wind and a burst of torrential rain. The gutters overflowed and the leaves dripped on the trees.

On just such a wintry evening, hail bounced and rattled against the Petersons' bedroom window and wind shook the ill-fitting frame, until Esther, goaded, ran for a newspaper to stuff the cracks. Wedging it in the spaces, she stood staring into the impenetrable blackness outside, allowing herself to be submerged.

The rain had stopped, but the extreme darkness, the howling wind and the intermittent splash it carried, signified that the storm had not yet reached its climax. The empty street shone wetly for a few feet under each high streetlight, and every isolated pool of electricity, by its feeble attempt to illumine infinity, made the night more desolate. The city clung to the edge of the land that sloped up from the bed of the sea: it sat on its asphalt mat: the asphalt mat clung to the hills where the natives had roamed.

Her conscious mind seeking supremacy, Esther was won back to action, and moved from the window absently. She crossed to the shoe cupboard and frowned into its depths, resuming the search that had been interrupted by the wind. The black suede court shoes. Yes. Do begin to think. They were what she wanted. Seeing them, a little chastened by her censor's irritation, she hurriedly lifted a straw mule out of the way, and a trickle of sand shot through her fingers to the floor.

In that instant she saw the turquoise waters of the North, felt the hot sand, smelt the salty, weedy, low-tide smell of the coastal town where she and Stan had idled for three perfect weeks. She allowed the sensations to take possession of her, feeling herself for a timeless moment into the receding spiral of the past. But then, abruptly, it was all effaced and she was back in the present, crouching over a thimbleful of sand, in a world that was colder and less bright.

Hurry, hurry. She, at least, must be on time at the Maitlands', for Stan would be late. He couldn't help it. Something very big was on just now: he disappeared at all hours of the day and night 'to see a man about a dog' he told her. But this, their first joint invitation from Laura, was an event; Esther hoped it would be successful. She wore a narrow velvet suit, black. She glanced at herself in the mirror and went downstairs.

Giving her a drink, Bill explained that Laura was still dressing. Anabel had been cross about going to bed. She had a slight temperature and it had taken longer than usual to get her settled for the night.

'And I warned Laura that Stan might be late. He's never quite sure when he'll be in, but he promised to make an effort tonight. Tell me,' she said, changing the subject before he could ask any questions, 'how is your house coming along? Is it almost finished?'

Bill said no, and brought out a bundle of photographs. 'In any case, we aren't going to live there except at weekends, you know. But it should be a good place for entertaining. Here there's hardly room for more than four extra people at a time, and you know how it is—the firm expects...'

He pointed. 'That's the games room. We'll be able to dance there. And that dilapidated corner beside the future rock garden is the future barbecue pit.' He grinned at her. 'I hope you're using your imagination.'

'You can tell from these,' she raised the photographs, 'that it's going to be very attractive indeed. And I think you must have one of the best sites on the harbour. We passed it in the car once when we were going, out to Palm Beach.'

'We'll have a view from every window.' He said it rather self-consciously, for it sounded like boasting, but the idea of a view from every window pleased him greatly.

Esther raised her eyebrows, impressed. 'But I didn't know you'd decided not to live there permanently?' she said.

Finishing his drink before he answered, Bill said, 'Well, it's a fair way out, you know. We thought we'd keep this place on until we can get around to a little car for Laura. She'd be cut off out there all day without one. But at the rate the building's going, I think we'll be set to move, new car and all, by the time it's finished.'

'We'll miss you,' Esther said.

'You and Stan should build on the next block and keep us company,' Bill said.

They turned to the plans again, and as Bill leaned close to her, pointing out details that she might not have appreciated, describing difficulties that had been overcome, Esther was restfully at ease, warmed by the log fire that burned in the grate, by the drink, by Bill's unassertive confidence and thoughtfulness.

And then Laura swept in, perfumed, beautifully made-up, her skirt rustling, her eyes shining. The night was made: the star had arrived and her presence guaranteed life enhancement for everyone in reach. She glowed: without dominating she guided. Esther caught from her an air of ease and soon they were all laughing. Bill was comfortably quiet, but admiration for his wife shone from him. He glanced now and then at Esther, the only other member of the audience, to assure himself that Laura was appreciated, and each time, seeing that she was, he relaxed and sank into enjoyment.

They talked about nothing in particular, for they had few, except public, personalities to discuss, and little else in common but age and propinquity. But it seemed enough, and it was—until Stan came in.

He accepted his drink and raised it and his eyebrows at Bill with a kind of glum significance. Two men against two women, he indicated. What was all this dressing-up about? Why the throaty chuckles— the expectant looks?

Seeing Esther's eyes on him, he sat forward in his chair and tried to pretend that he was listening and interested. Tried to pretend—it was as far from convincing as that.

Bill swallowed his rage at the insult to Laura, and she, too, though contemptuous and bored by Stan's lack of *savoir faire*, was outwardly unaffected. Esther guessed something at their reactions and could sympathise, even as her liking for them deteriorated in the face of their well-hidden disapproval. For Stan's uncouth behaviour she felt a mixture of pity and hopelessness.

'Hmm. Mmm.' Stan would clear his throat and act as if the noise he made had some bearing on the conversation, as if the tone indicated intelligent agreement or reasoned opposition.

If there was a flurry of laughter, he would notice that the three faces in front of his had turned up their mouths, that the skin at the corners of their eyes had crinkled, that their bodies shook very slightly at the shoulders, and then, ten seconds too late, his mouth and eyes and shoulders moved in imitation.

Bill tried business, finance, horses, golf, the weather, and finally, with an apologetic glance at Esther, their own new house. Then Laura and Esther took over. Eating steadily through the excellent dinner Stan answered, 'Yeah...yeah.' Even the numerous drinks that Bill poured hopefully for him had no loosening effect. He became more morose and bothered less to hide it as the night wore on.

When at last it was over, and the Maitlands were alone in their flat, they gazed at one another with anger and relief.

'My God!' Bill stormed over to the drink tray. 'Never again! God, what a night! What's the matter with that character? Here you are, angel.' He handed her another drink, and Laura began to laugh.

After frowning into his glass for a while, Bill joined in. He wiped his forehead with an exaggerated gesture. 'God!' he said again. 'How could she have married him? Do you think he's usually as bad as that? Or has he got something special against us, do you suppose?'

Laura said, 'Come here,' and Bill leaned over and kissed her. 'You've seen more of him than I have. It was just what I expected. I thought it would be interesting to see them together, though; that's why I asked them.' She pushed Bill's hair back from his forehead.

'Well, it was!' he said emphatically.

'Oh, now, darling,' she teased, 'she has improved him a bit. Really. The poor dope was just in a bad way tonight.'

Bill shook his head. 'I don't know. Maybe she has. Maybe she likes her men that way. I think you're right, though—he must have something on his mind.'

At this understatement laughter swept over them again. Laura groaned, exhausted. 'Maybe!' she repeated. Then, more seriously, she said, 'But did you notice the way he looked when I took them in to see Anabel?'

'Oh, I think he likes kids all right,' Bill admitted reluctantly.

'But she did look sweet, darling, didn't she? The lamb. Come here, angel,' her voice deepened, she held up her arms.

Upstairs, Stan sat with his head in his hands while Esther, on the arm of his chair, watching him, lit two cigarettes and put one between his fingers. Stan dragged at it and, after exhaling, lifted his head. 'Yap, yap, yap! If she doesn't think she's it!' He closed his eyes with disgust and opened them quickly again to warn: 'I'm not going down there again. If you want to—okay— that's fine with me. Just leave me out of it.'

Esther got up to pull the curtains across the windows. It was raining hard. She held her cigarette in her left hand while she reached up, smoothly guiding the material as it shut out the cold black glass. She switched on the radiator and the table lamp.

'If someone knocks at the door tonight, don't answer it.'

She had been at the mantelpiece, tipping ash from her cigarette. Now she turned slowly, amazed by his change of subject, and eyes met, alone, for the first time that night.

'Why?'

'Because I say so.'

'Tell me what's wrong.' She was startled, and her voice, where she meant to be calm, was sharp. 'Please,' she insisted. 'If there's anything wrong, Stan, I want to know. Surely—' she stopped abruptly, not wanting to say too much.

Stan sighed heavily and heaved himself about in his chair. 'Sure, sure.'

She thought: He's going to tell me.

'But I don't know what you're all excited about. It's only business. You wouldn't understand about it, pet. Everything's okay, if you just do what Stan tells you.'

Her mild resentment went with an inaudible sigh. She sat down. 'All right.'

'There's one thing, though—I could do with a drink.' Stan waited, but Esther remained still, so he lumbered into the kitchen himself and raked in the cupboard. Coming back, his glass in his hand, he sat on the floor with his back against her legs.

Automatically, Esther smoothed his hair. The light, soothing pressure of fingers on scalp gave him a momentary sense of peace, but almost at once it flickered out. He was swamped by a dreary, restless despair. He felt old. Time went too fast. Life wasn't funny any more. What was it all about, anyway?

He drained his glass and wiped his mouth with the back of his hand.

'Everything will be all right. You'll feel better soon,' Esther said gently, not caring if he drank too much.

Yeah, like hell, he thought. Much you know.

He caught her hand, laced her fingers through his, studied the skin, pressed the bone. It was a long, fine hand. He dropped it discontentedly.

'I better get that dough tomorrow,' he said suddenly.

'What do you mean?'

'For this cove that's coming.'

Esther looked puzzled, but did not question him and he smiled at her quite tenderly and yawned. 'Think we ought to turn in now, petty?'

'Can we?'

'Sure. Why not? It's late. It's damn chilly, too.'

That was true: although the radiator burned with ugly orange heat, after the Maitlands' heaped-up logs it seemed ineffective and tawdry.

Stan went into the kitchen with his glass, came back and stubbed out his cigarette. Esther lifted her small velvet bag and touched the pile with one finger.

There came three sharp raps on the front door. Esther and Stan stood motionless, jerked to attention.

'It's okay. Stay there. The light won't show under the door.' An alert, tight smile appeared on his face.

Eyes opened wide, lips parted, Esther listened with all her senses and heard only the pounding of her heart.

Again there were three raps.

Stan turned his smiling, listening face on her, asking her to share his pleasure.

'Do you know who it is?' she whispered.

'Course! It's only the cove I told you about. I'll see him tomorrow, when I've got the cash.'

'But what does he want? Why don't you see him and tell him you'll have it tomorrow?'

99

'No need to worry, Est.' Stan's tone was excessively soothing. 'He'll do a bunk in a minute. Anyway, he's harmless. He's going to give us a bit of a hand.'

'How?'

'Oh,' his expression cryptic, maddening, he said, 'he just knows a man who knows a man…'

CHAPTER ELEVEN

He didn't know how Vi came back into his life: no conscious wish, no intention, had been allowed to reach the surface of his mind, but it happened one day that instead of bypassing the Cross Keys, as he had for months, he went in.

It was morning and the place was quiet. Joe stood at the end of the dimly lit bar polishing glasses with a dry towel. He lifted his head as the door swung shut. After a moment he said, 'Hi!' casually, unsurprised. A cigarette hung from the corner of his mouth. He returned to his polishing, but as Stan walked slowly over to him their eyes never parted. Their looks were their conversation. Leaning heavily on the bar, Stan pursed his lips: Joe raised his brows and Stan shook his head.

There was a prolonged boom of thunder and the long mirror backing the bar flared for an instant, reflecting the sheet lightning that hung in the sulphurous sky outside.

'She's out the back.' Joe jerked his head. He moved to the other end of the bar.

Stan looked in three rooms before he found her. They were private drinking parlours, dark and dismal, with browny varnished walls and linoleum floors; each furnished with a leatherette sofa, four wooden chairs and a table—unprepossessing. But the sight of the familiar squalor, reminding him of the past, struck Stan so keenly that he could no longer hide from himself the urgency of his desire to see her again. As he strode down the corridor to the next room his face was grim. He opened the fourth door and saw her standing at the window looking out at the rain, an empty tray hanging in one hand.

Jolted, he thought: Here she is. What now? He was almost surprised to find that she still existed, that her life had gone on all these months; that Vi, whose face he knew as well as his own, stood at the window staring at the rain.

'Hiya, captain!' he said, striving for jocularity.

There was a silence deeper than silence in the room—a suspension of life. When, seconds later, she could think and move, Vi was aware that a stronger current of life returned to her than had been halted.

Stan had come back. Although she had not turned or looked at him, her body was heavy with the knowledge of his presence. The load of ice at her heart had gone, leaving no trace, making her seem by its complete absence almost deprived, a stranger to the self she had grown to know.

Glancing round at him, her eyes were hard.

'Still got a voice?' He lounged awkwardly in the doorway, grinning. 'How've you been?'

'Oh, fine. Just fine.'

Holding out his cigarette case, Stan came towards her, but she shook her head, took one from a packet she had in her pocket, and lit it herself. She was glad then, to sit down. The first spasm of joy had vanished, and her heart was beating with quick, excited bitterness: a bitterness that had been repressed with stoic determination in the early days of his desertion.

Stan looked around, smoking restlessly. 'Joe ought to get this place done up. It looks like hell.'

'You've said that before.'

'He ought to tear those old fireplaces out.'

'I'll tell him for you.' After a pause she said in a different voice, 'I suppose this is where we say, "It's been a long time" and all that. Or isn't that why you've come?'

Stan twisted uncomfortably on his chair. 'Oh, hell! Don't start anything, Vi—forget it. I'm here now, aren't I?'

She knew all about it: some of the boys told her a few days after it happened. Why keep on about it?

She looked away, and Stan's eyes went surreptitiously over the heavy blonde hair, the firm fine skin of her face, the wide mouth, the full curve of her bust at the top of her low-necked dress.

'Come on, come on!' he rallied her, thickly. 'Loosen up, why don't you?'

Vi gave a short laugh. 'Yeah, I'll loosen up, all right.'

He glared at her belligerently until he saw that he was not secure enough for a show of huffy pride or anger. And he was moved by her closeness: he could not go away. He was tied to her by a thousand strands of memory.

'I'll get some drinks,' he said, and she looked at him without speaking, so he went to the bar.

Alone, Vi sat motionless. She would take him back. There was no decision to be made. He had come, and it looked as if she could have him again if she wanted him—and she did. She did. Then why this angry pain, this flat despair? They would have been appropriate months ago, not now.

It was simply, she supposed, that this time he had done his worst—touched the limit. His going had not revealed what his return immediately made clear. Not one illusion stood.

And yet, some sad quality of life, necessary to her, depended wholly on his presence, words and actions.

Under the compound shock of loss and gain, she sat staring at the wooden table, waiting for him. There was a cold acceptance of the facts, a final renunciation, then a deliberate and quite genuine lifting of her heart.

Stabbing at the battered tin ashtray with her cigarette, she said to herself: You dope, you silly dope; apparently scornful, in fact approving, meaning: Yes, this is the way. This is the only thing.

She heard his footsteps in the passage and her mascaraed lashes flickered over deep blue eyes. They drank together and then she smiled at him. Stan saw the even white teeth, the old familiar expression, and the tension went from his body. He slumped loosely, relieved, but quickly complacent.

'Well'—he almost rubbed his hands together—'well, what's the news, kiddo?'

She shook her head at his masculine lack of subtlety and laughed aloud while Stan looked at her, eager to respond, not understanding.

'My God, you've worn well,' he told her. 'You're not a bad-looking dame.'

Her mouth curled in appreciation of the compliment. She knew that her looks had not diminished. She had been born to be forty: it was her time. At forty she was more attractive than she had been at twenty, and much hard-earned knowledge had been added to her natural good-humoured charm.

'What's the news?' Stan asked again, putting his feet up on another chair. 'I haven't heard anything for weeks.'

A cold silence, hung with a dozen unspoken retorts, fell between them.

Swirling the remainder of her beer in the bottom of the glass, Vi said mechanically, 'Let's see. What's new?' Her heart thudded dully. When a few scraps of gossip swam like jellyfish into her mind she caught them gratefully. A moment later, transformed into rainbow-coloured aquarium pieces, they sped forth to dazzle Stan.

The morose listening mask of his face lightened gradually as the narration turned into a performance, which, because it was for him, was exceptionally good, even for Vi. They laughed themselves back to silence.

'Oh dear,' Vi smiled and smoothed her dress.

Stan snorted through his nose. He had forgotten what great company she was. When a man was with her he felt alive.

There was another crash of thunder outside, and a chilly draught swept round them. They turned their heads to the window abstractedly, stared blindly at the grey glass panes.

Less spontaneous now, Vi said, 'Oh, did you know Nobby and Jock have disappeared? Few weeks ago. They'll turn up again, but Eck says he hopes they stay lost. They put him on to a dead horse and he lost a packet. He found out they were on something else, too.'

'Huh! Serves the silly cow right!'

'And old Potty—got a smoke, Stan?—he's in again.'

'What for this time?'

'Thanks.' She removed a piece of tobacco from her tongue with a long red fingernail. 'Same as usual. Poor old Pot—he'll never learn.'

Through the screen of cigarette smoke their eyes made contact, sheered off again like startled birds, and then returned.

Vi drew in a deep breath, let it escape slowly and stubbed out her cigarette. She looked at her watch. It was a small platinum one, a present from Stan. They remembered this, and the occasion of its giving, simultaneously, and both stood up.

'What about—' Stan began.

'I'll have to go in a minute...I've got to see what they're doing in the kitchen. We're short-staffed this week.' Her eyes were wide, her mouth drooped pathetically, expectantly. 'What were you going to say?'

He caught her arms and gave her a hard, lingering kiss, holding her tight until at last, breathless, she pushed him away.

'Why here and now, of all times and places?'

Silently, he took her again and kissed her with an insistence that made her strain against him and, a moment later, break away.

'You'll be in tonight.' It was a statement.

'Yes.'

'You don't sound very keen. Perhaps you'd like it better if I didn't bother?'

She said shortly, 'You can please yourself about that. I'm going now.'

Alarmed, he was immediately ingratiating. 'I was only kidding—you know me.'

'Yeah. One great clown, aren't you?'

He stood in front of the closed door, feeling masculine and masterful.

'Come on,' Vi said, 'let me out.' She was all at once tired and jangled and she wanted to be away from him.

'Say you're glad to see me,' he wheedled with unnatural jocularity.

Standing close to him she said, with a faint smile, 'He wants me to tell him.' She gave his arm a little push. 'Come on, let me out.'

Reluctantly he let her go, and stood for a moment afterwards, listening to the echo of her high-heeled shoes in the bare, beery corridor.

When he went out he raised his hand significantly to Joe like a diplomat who has come home with the treaty signed.

It's on again. We're back together.

In the street it was cold. The light in the sky was still lurid and threatening, for the storm had not broken in force. The wind blew the soft brim of Stan's hat out of shape. Without his car, which was at Cooper's for an overhaul, he felt peculiarly vulnerable, as though, on foot, he might be overtaken and killed by enemies.

A sleek black-and-silver taxi cruised up one side of the street and down the other. Leo Schmidt was having a poor day—that is, one slightly less successful than yesterday which had been, as usual, a bonanza.

'There's not enough dough floatin' about,' he complained to his wife at dinner. 'The country's goin' to the dogs. It's the ruddy government. Now if we was in Russia'—he paused over his steak—'it'd be different.'

'How?' his wife asked.

'For God's sake, don't nag! Just different.'

Stan hailed the cab. He gave his order curtly and settled back on the well-sprung seat to review his meeting with Vi. He bit nervously at a jagged fingernail.

'I *said*, Mister, do you want a tip for Saturday?'

Catching the sense without hearing the words, Stan glanced up at the driver's mirror. 'No!'

'Okay. Okay. Keep your hair on!'

Everything's all right, Stan congratulated himself. She never expected anything for herself. She doesn't hold it against me. No reason why she should. She's a sensible kid. And a lot more. But what about Est? She wouldn't be too keen on it if she knew.

The banal wording of his thought, the understatement, gave him a twinge, and he gazed uneasily out of the window at the dull brick bungalows and small suburban food shops.

Well, she won't know, he decided, so it won't make any diff to her or the way I am about her. She knows things about me I'd never tell Vi in a million years. What's between us—it's different. A man and his wife.

It sounded good and solid.

Yes, but you can't let old friends down. A pal like Vi you can't just dump. Vi. Vi...

Her name went round and round in his brain, leading the way to a suspicion he had been searching for. Now, she hadn't been by herself all this time. Not Vi. He began to wonder who she might have been seeing. Joe, maybe. No. He was pretty well occupied. But someone.

There was a foul taste in his mouth. He screwed down the window and spat.

The taxi dropped him at Jeffries' cracked and peeling gate. While he searched in his pockets for change he gazed dispassionately up and down the barren asphalt road, at the rows of semi-detached single-storied houses of dark red brick. The dim light of day could not pierce the narrow windows of the houses, and electric light glowed feebly at scattered points along the street. As Stan fumbled with the unfamiliar gate catch, a greasy sheet of newspaper whipped from the gutter and clung to his legs: cursing, he freed himself and made his way round to the side door.

110

In the kitchen, over tea and baked beans, the two men discussed the arrangements for Jeffries' forthcoming trip to Melbourne. The ex-gardener had proved himself as able as any of the boys who travelled for Stan, and in a comparatively short time had been made responsible for organising the manufacture of machine parts in other states.

'You don't want to hump manure and dig holes all your days,' Stan had said to him at the beginning, not adding, as he might, 'You know too much. It doesn't suit me to have you working for the Prescotts.' But Jeffries had understood, and both men profited by the new agreement.

In the early afternoon, the business completed, Stan caught a taxi to the Bridge Heights Hotel, where he stayed for the rest of the day, sitting by himself. At last, rousing himself to go home, he hailed another taxi, and, paying his fare grudgingly, stepped from the car with alcoholic carefulness.

Brooding over the luck of a car owner who had in one day paid three cab fares, he said to a passerby, 'These coves are making a fortune.'

The sound of his voice, the shocked face of the middle-aged woman he had addressed, told him that he was rather drunk, but to prove the scientific truth of his theory that whisky cleared the brain, he ran swiftly, diagonally, up the entrance stairs of Romney Court.

111

Esther heard him at the door and hurried to let him in. When she saw his face she thought with relief that David, whom she had managed to push out of the flat half an hour earlier, would now be some miles away.

'Hello, darling. I'm only in for about half an hour,' he sighed. 'Have to meet the boys again later. Work, work, work.' He attempted a rueful laugh.

'Oh, must you?' But she didn't protest seriously, knowing that much of his business was done at night.

They went through to the dining room, and Stan blinked owlishly at the lighted candles that burned on the table. His reactions were unusually slow.

'What-ho!…A celebration?' he hazarded.

'No, but I thought candles would look cheerful on such a miserable night. It's so bleak outside.'

'Very cheerful,' he said, nodding his head, thinking of Vi and feeling a little sad and indulgent towards Esther. 'Sorry, pet.' He looked at her sheepishly. 'I think I had a bit too much at the pub this evening. Sorry.'

His admission somehow had the effect of making her feel safe and protective. And while he sat down and shook his head experimentally, she went to the kitchen, tranquil, humming a tune.

Lowering the gas jets under the vegetables, she served the soup and put the pot in the sink to soak. As she carried the plates in and set them on the table she said, 'David called in this afternoon. Just to see how I was,' she added when Stan made no comment.

After a long pause he said, 'Oh, *did* he?' and the weight of hostile insinuation in his voice made her freeze. 'Checking up on his low-class brother-in-law, was he?'

'Oh, Stan,' she began hopelessly, and stopped. 'Here is your soup, pet. Come, have it while it's hot. It will make you feel better.' She looked at him across the room and raised her eyebrows appealingly. 'I think I'll start. I'm hungry.'

He mocked, 'Starting without me! Dear, dear! What manners! I thought you knew better than that, my dear Esther. Your poor ignorant husband expects you to show him the right way to do things, and here...'

The candlelight threw shadows on Esther's face as she stared at him, expressionless with apprehension. The light gleamed on the embroidery of her black cashmere sweater, flickered in the creamy depths of the soup she could not eat.

Stan muttered to himself, 'Me sayin' I'm sorry to her because a man's had a drink on a cold day to get warm.'

'And what did our friend David have to say for himself, eh?...Eh?'

Esther knelt on the floor beside his chair. 'Stan, listen. I love you.'

113

What else? What other words could she say? Encircled by his animosity, a kind of frustrated speech-lessness lodged in her chest, she felt the inadequacy of words as a means of breaking through to him. Language was no link between species. 'Everyone belonging to me likes and admires you for yourself, Stan. I wish you'd believe me. I wish you would.'

The theatrical quality of the scene appalled her, and suddenly she turned away.

Stan had seldom seen Esther cry, and her tears had never gratified him more. They put her in the wrong, made his defection very understandable. At the same time, he complained, 'So this is the high-and-mighty thing I married!'

After a few minutes he saw that she had stopped crying. The thought filtered through to his muddled senses that she had never looked more splendid. The thin face, the grey eyes, her expression...What was her expression? He gazed at her interestedly, but he could not define it. It was Esther's face and it looked serious, or sad, or something—further than that he would not go. In spite of the tears there was quality there—the real thing. For a moment he was smugly content that he possessed quality, that he had upset quality.

'What are you trying to do, Stan?'

He waved a supercilious hand. 'Nothing. Nothing at all.' Something had deflated inside him. Not knowing what else to do, he went into the bathroom and let the cold shower run over his head. Water soaked through his collar, ran down his chest, splashed the shoulders of his coat.

At length he turned off the tap, dried his face and combed his hair. He threw his coat into the hall cupboard and dragged a woollen pullover on top of his damp shirt.

The unfamiliar candles, still burning, caught his eye when he went back to the other room. Esther looked up at him as he stood in the doorway, dumb.

'Will you have some dinner now?'

He held up his hands and dropped them. 'Please.'

When they sat down he said, 'I don't know why I do it. No use saying I'm sorry if I keep on doing it.' He put his elbows on the table, his head in his hands.

She spoke quickly, almost pettishly, remembering her thoughts but not her feeling. 'You must hate me, Stan, when you want so badly to humiliate me. You can't want to hurt someone you love. Can you?'

'Oh, God!' Stan groaned, and poured some brandy for her. 'Drink it!' he said. He watched her for a minute more, opened his mouth to speak but, finding no words, stuffed his hands in his pockets and strode onto the balcony.

The night was black and there was a high wind. His eyes saw the dark outlines of buildings, their windows lighted. He saw the streetlights, solitary beacons, the lights on the harbour bridge. He had seen it all a thousand times before. He thought of Vi and cursed under his breath, impatiently.

'Est,' he said, going back into the room. 'It didn't mean anything. I just had a bit too much. I can't even remember what it was all about.'

Neither could Esther catch a sentence, remember a phrase to justify her own outburst, the unrestraint she hated.

Should she have been indifferent? she wondered. She didn't know. But something in her was outraged. It was not a question of reason. A quarrel crushed life and time, left no person innocent.

'Why don't you yell at me or something?' Stan demanded, exasperated. He moved round behind her chair and put his hands on her shoulders. 'I didn't mean anything, Est. I don't know what I'd do...'

His protestations sounded flat and unconvincing even to his own ears. And Esther wondered why anger and abuse should be so richly stimulating, why they should have the seal of genuine feeling, while sorrow and regret have the tasteless quality of watered milk—unsatisfactory alike to those who offer and those who receive.

Without turning, she said, 'I know.' Then she straightened her finely pleated skirt, and said, 'I think my hair must be standing on end. I must fix it.'

Through globules and spangles of cold water she saw, as she splashed her face, the frieze of blue-tiled fish swimming round the green-tiled sea of the bathroom wall. Once, in a rare mood of light-heartedness, Stan had christened them.

'The only pets we've space for,' he had said. 'Leo and Cleo, Arthur and Martha, Dover and Clover...'

She identified them automatically while she cleaned her face and applied new make-up.

'I've reheated the soup, Est.' Stan came out of the kitchen as she returned. He gave her arm a squeeze. 'You look great,' he said heartily, his mouth smiling widely.

'That's good,' she said. It seemed to answer both declarations. She blew out the candles and carried them, one in each hand, dark red candles trailing frail banners of smoke, to the sideboard. Before sitting down she switched on the wireless and stood looking at the lighted panel as she turned the dial in search of music.

Stan glanced at his watch and thought again of Vi. This carry-on had lasted long enough. It was ten past seven. He could leave in about ten minutes and be with her by half-past. He began scooping up his soup: he swallowed the overdone roast in chunks and said he would give coffee a miss.

After changing his damp shirt he came back to say goodbye. 'You should see if young Rachel'll go to the pictures with you,' he said. 'You'd be in good time for the eight o'clock session.'

Walking to the door with him, Esther said she probably would.

'I'll be pretty late.' Stan shrugged into his overcoat. 'You'd better not wait up for me, pet. Damn and blast having to go out on a night like this. If they were all worth their salt they could manage things without me there. Haven't got a brain between them.' He kissed her on the cheek and went.

CHAPTER TWELVE

The small swimming pools staked out like oyster beds at various points inside the harbour are not admired by those who have close access to the beaches of the many ocean suburbs. The pools have neither the clear sandy floor nor the rolling breakers of the beaches, and instead of yellow sifted sand, sunbathers must lie on gritty salt-and-pepper shingle. But, since they are frequented, for convenience's sake, by dwellers on the fashionable south side of the harbour, the pools acquire a certain social distinction.

All winter long these fenced-in patches of harbour water and shingle lie forlorn, deserted by all except the few energetic elderly men who exercise and swim regardless of temperature.

But now, although one week might hold a day that

looked like summer, and another like winter, it was really spring: a spring heralded in the seasonless land by some lines in a newspaper, and not, as in others, by the slow unfolding of the apple-green umbrella of the trees.

Having read the news and bought her summer clothes, Laura Maitland decided that the time had come to begin her pilgrimages to the pool with Anabel. It was not that Laura liked to swim—she did not. Nor had she any interest in the pleasures of burning fair skin, oiling, peeling, burning, and finally turning a shade darker than she was by nature intended to be. But for Anabel's sake, she had last night decided, it was her duty to be at the right place at the right time. Anabel was friendly. Some of *their* children were bound to be friendly. It stood to reason that, given the assistance of time, luck, and the law of averages, she herself was certain to have an opportunity for conversation: after that she would need no further help from fate.

But, passing the morning, its motives and results, through the astringent test of her own self-knowledge, Laura shook her head. Did she really want, or want Anabel, to be friends with the habitués of the pool? They had been there this morning in a group, looking long and lean and brown, cool and hard-eyed. They were smarter than Americans, prettier than the English. To them a broken fingernail, the first grey hair, was worse than death. It was unlikely, Laura thought, that they believed in death at all. One had money, one was smart, one lived in Sydney, one was immortal and so was one's youth.

Laura smiled a little. She believed in death, but she believed in life. She believed in the heart. When she went back to the pool it would be because it had water and sand and Anabel liked both.

She was walking up the hill, pushing Anabel's stroller towards the park where they would wait for Esther. They passed the bright, expensive food shops, the chemist's shop with its heavy air of French perfume, and gazed for a moment at the window where Madame Didet was showing a hat from her new collection.

From the canvas stroller came the chant: 'Anabel got a shell! Anabel got a shell!'

As she moved on, Laura's smile was strained. Anabel had been having her shell on and off for three-quarters of an hour. 'All right, darling,' she crooned. 'We'll soon meet Auntie Esther, get Anabel a nice big drink of milk.'

She smiled modestly but gaily at a woman who stopped to compliment her on Anabel's sweet face.

'There's a good girl,' she said.

'Anabel got a shell! An-a-bel—'

'Oh, please, darling!'

'Hello, Mrs Maitland.'

Laura glanced round sharply. 'Rachel! Goodness, you seem to have grown. I hardly knew you. Why are you wearing a coat, today? It's spring.'

'Is it? I felt cold.' She dropped to the side of the stroller to kiss Anabel. 'Hello, sweetie. Oh, you are a dear baby,' she teased, smiling at the little girl, delighted to see her.

'And where are you off to this morning, Rae? I haven't seen you for weeks.'

'I'm going to do some shopping—into town. Saturday morning's the only chance I have.'

They fell into step and walked on slowly, Anabel craning round to catch Rachel's attention.

'I've really missed you, Rachel,' Laura said. 'And I've been hurt, too. I think you've been staying away deliberately because you don't want to see me. I don't know what I've done to deserve this kind of treatment from you.'

A soothing, not disagreeable, sadness swept over Rachel as she heard this, and she thought how effectively Laura called up this emotion. She guessed that Laura's feeling was genuine as spoke, even if the scene and its result were calculated, and her own feeling beat true, too, in spite of a subterranean resistance to being conquered.

'I'm sorry,' Rachel said, remembering past kindness, remembering that Laura alone had noticed she was unhappy, and that she had sometimes cared, which, short of performing a miracle, seemed now the most and best she could have done.

They were separated by a group of people who

stood talking in the middle of the footpath. Rachel could hear Anabel's urgent cry. 'Rae! Rae!'

They came together again and Anabel was pacified, her attention soon caught by the sight of a gleaming Irish setter prancing along in front of her. Laura had stopped to wait for Rachel, and for just a second before they moved on, she turned her glorious eyes on the girl.

'I don't want you to apologise to me, Rae. But come up to see us sometimes after work. It doesn't matter if Bill's there. He likes to see you, too. And as for Anabel—well, she's been asking for you nonstop for weeks.'

'I'm sorry,' Rachel said again, and Laura smiled at her with a glint of her old humour.

Rachel knew the expression: it signalled forgiveness and friendship and made her spirits soar, for no amount of critical analysis could alter the fact that, whatever else she was, Laura was wonderful.

They had reached the small public park at the end of the shopping centre, and as Laura manoeuvred the stroller onto the path, she said, all boisterous charm now, 'What's all this about going into town? You can't run away like that. Sit down and talk until Esther comes along, and then have coffee with us at the Casablanca.'

Wrinkling her brow, Rachel looked at her watch. 'It's awfully late and I'm desperate for shoes,' she wailed with the youthful abandon that Laura liked to see.

The older woman smiled and shielded her eyes from the sun as she watched Rachel's show of indecision.

'Come on!' she said, knowing she would have her way, and went on down the path. 'Esther and Anabel are great friends now,' she called. 'Wait till you see! You'll be jealous.'

The park, which was square, had flowerbeds at each corner, and was dissected by two long paths into four smaller squares. At the junction stood a piece of sculpture, the subject of many and much juvenile delight, for the unidentifiable protuberances that chafed the aldermen were a joy to small rock-climbers.

Unfastening the straps that held her daughter in the stroller, Laura leaned back on the seat and watched her running unsteadily to join a group of children who were playing with a ball.

'One piece of news I've had from your aunt is that you're going out with an Italian.' She raised her voice on the last word in the manner of a counsel for the prosecution. With a long fingernail she flaked red polish from another nail. Her arms felt cold.

Rachel pressed her lips together. 'Yes,' she said, and thought of Luigi Robérto, whom she had met at work. A former classics master from Milan, he was twenty-seven, and had been in Sydney for three years.

Laura's eyes narrowed with triumph as she dislodged a piece of polish that had clung to her nail like cement. 'There's no doubt you're a different girl since you took this job,' she said, tacking round the subject, her absorption in her fingernails giving her voice a tight abstracted note. 'As long as it doesn't make you forget all your old friends, I'd say I was very happy about it.' She abandoned her surface mining operations and clasped her hands together.

All my old friends! Rachel looked at the sky.

The children were calling to one another in high, excited voices. Laura heard Anabel shriek as the ball fell into her hands.

Turning again to the girl, Laura said, 'While I've got you here, darling, I want you to promise me something.' She paused. 'I want you to promise that you won't get too deeply involved with this Italian. I don't mind telling you, Rae, I'm surprised your aunt hasn't put a stop to it.'

Anger tore like a whirlwind through Rachel's chest, and echoes of her recent appraisal of Laura lent it strength.

'After all, dear,' misled by her silence, Laura continued, 'what do you know about him?'

'Quite a lot,' Rachel said stonily: that he had knowledge, that he treated her as an adult, and liked her to say what she thought. She knew that he was working to bring his mother and sister from Milan. 'Quite a lot,' Rachel said, and Laura stopped, but decided to ignore the challenge in her voice.

'I know you've been lonely, and I think every young girl should have her boy friends. But a foreigner!—I

125

won't call him a new Australian—I don't suppose he's even naturalised. They come here and take the good things we have to offer and they don't even want to become citizens.' For a moment she was almost diverted to the fall of the Empire, but she saw in time that its introduction would be inartistic. 'What do you say?' she asked, when Rachel was silent. 'I know you won't like this plain-speaking, dear, but I talk to you like this because I'm fond of you. Don't be taken in by your friend's polite manners. You won't remember what the Italians did to the Abyssinians, but I can tell you they weren't so charming then. You wouldn't think so much of this friend of yours if you knew all that I know about the Italians, my dear little girl.'

Rachel was at home accustomed to a certain amount of ridicule: she had trained herself to listen objectively and test the accuracy of the charges against her. But that Luigi should be attacked because of her, made her despair.

In the old dependent days, afraid as she was of exile, she had never dared to answer Laura truthfully if that meant contradiction, but now, trying to control her uneven breathing, she said stiltedly, 'I know you're thinking of me, Mrs Maitland, but generalisations about national characteristics, or anything else, are so pointless as a rule. Luigi's only one Italian. He's very nice, and you've never met him, so how can you warn me against him?'

Laura recoiled. 'How dare you take that tone to me, Rachel! You're a very silly ungrateful little girl and I really wonder why I bother with you at all.'

To her astonishment, for she never cried by accident, tears of mortification came to her eyes. Apart from having a word like 'generalisations' thrown at her, the unparalleled revolt had upset her badly. At her side Rachel, not less astonished by her utterance and her daring, sat quite frozen.

While Laura searched for a handkerchief, Rachel, horrified to see her tears, had to blink rapidly to keep back her own. Loyalty had never seemed more complex.

'I never thought you'd speak to me like that, Rachel,' Laura said in a voice so grave that the girl had to force herself to meet her eyes.

'I didn't say it to...'

'What you intended, I don't know. But you spoke rudely to me for the first time since I've known you, and it's very hurtful indeed to see that you think so little of me. That man's been filling your head with ideas. It's what I thought would happen. He's changed you. He's probably a communist.'

Misery vanished, and, looking away from Laura, Rachel rolled her eyes. She thought if it went on much longer she would disintegrate.

At that moment Laura saw Esther, and a slight frown appeared on her face. Esther was saying goodbye to a fair, well-dressed woman who seemed, as she stared, increasingly familiar. She puzzled for a moment, and it came. Impatiently she tapped at Rachel's arm. 'Wasn't that girl Angela Ford before she married? She was terribly well known when she was a deb. I've seen a million photos of her. Her people are rolling.'

But Rachel was no help. She didn't know. When Esther joined them she left to go to town almost at once.

'Oh, goodbye, Rae,' Laura said vaguely. And as she walked away, Rachel heard her say, 'Wasn't that Angela Ford you were talking to just now?'

'Angela Prescott now. She's my sister-in-law—my brother Hector's wife,' Esther said.

'Well, well, well. Imagine that!' Laura smiled. 'I thought I recognised her face.' And, still smiling, she called Anabel and strapped her back into the stroller.

In the smart, crowded Casablanca half an hour later, she remembered Rachel and said, 'I was having a dreadful time with that young pal of ours this morning.'

'Oh?' Esther was noncommittal: she thought if it was true, it was a healthy sign of independence on Rachel's part.

'It was about this Italian boy friend of hers.'

'You've met him, too?' Esther asked.

'No...'

'I have. One night last week. I thought he seemed particularly nice—exactly the right sort of person for Rachel. I was so pleased.'

'Oh?' Laura turned to Anabel. 'Have another biscuit, darling? There's a good girl. Cigarette?' She held out her case to Esther, and when they were both smoking she smiled and turned again to her daughter. 'Doesn't Auntie Esther think Anabel's a good girl, sitting there so nicely all this time?'

CHAPTER THIRTEEN

The ceiling was thick with flies. Esther gazed at them with passive disgust for a while and then went to grope in the cupboard for the fly spray.

Her hand brushed over a jagged tin as it lifted the spray from the clutter, and, as she straightened up, she saw blood oozing with poisonous slowness from a long tear across the joint of her thumb. She looked at it indifferently, then, rousing herself, turned on the cold-water tap, squeezed the wound and held it under the clear glugging funnel of water. She dabbed it with iodine, and managed to tie one of Stan's big handkerchiefs around the joint, knotting it at her wrist.

Trailing in to the other room with the spray, she started to push the plunger, releasing the disinfectant, which rose in a strong-smelling mist, disturbing the black colony of flies, and fell again in a damp cloud on her head and shoulders. She held her breath as long as she could, and then, with a final burst of the spray, dashed onto the balcony, and gasped the air with relief.

It was hot. The sky was near white, heat-hazy, dazzling. It was a boring heat that muffled sound and slowed movement. The air that had seemed clean a moment before was dusty and humid. Her hair clung damply to her scalp. She would need a shower after bathing in insecticide.

She leaned on the balcony and looked out. She supposed, but hardly believed, that people were working somewhere out there: canning food, sewing clothes, making steel, while machines clanged victoriously, impervious to heat.

Hector, Clem and David all worked in cool, straight buildings, air-conditioned, marble-staired, high-ceilinged. And Stan—he could be anywhere.

The straw mules on her bare feet flap-flapped as she went to the bedroom to find some clean clothes, a thinner dress, then flap-flapped into the bathroom.

The cold tap three-quarters, and the hot, one. She tested the result and stepped onto the tiled floor of the shower recess. The soft warm water ran over her head, into her ears, over her face. She gave a groan of satisfaction as the heat left her skin. After she had washed herself, she shampooed her hair, automatically, while some thought, some memory, hovered dreamlike in her mind, just out of sight.

She dressed slowly, wondering what it was, not wanting to know, compelled, at last, to drag it from the hidey-hole.

Oh, yes. That was it. How could she have forgotten?

In self-defence her face assumed a wry expression to show to the mirror, but even so, she felt a little sick.

That doctor this morning—a Macquarie Street specialist, so he knew what he was doing—no children, he said.

She saw his face again as he talked to her afterwards, pale, smooth-skinned, steady eyes. He had been very kind.

Dr Burton-Travers. He has a good reputation. No children...Well, it doesn't matter. He said we can always adopt one if we want to. But Stan doesn't want children...At least, he said right at the beginning that we wouldn't want one yet. But I think he was making sure that I didn't, at all. And neither I do. I only thought it might...

She dried her hair again, vigorously, with a fresh towel, and then combed it, determinedly avoiding her eyes in the mirror. I'm glad my hair curls naturally, she thought. It's a relief to be able to wash it on a day like this. With a firm hand she applied lipstick to her pale mouth.

I don't know why I went, she thought, as she lay

back on the long chair on the balcony. I've never thought about children. It was simply that I thought it might help Stan. I don't know how or why.

She turned her head from side to side and closed her eyes. Stan's not the kind of man who wants his own house in the suburbs, and children at school, and responsibilities. I don't either. I like flat life. I want things to go on exactly as they are.

Esther had no picture of a different, ideal life, hanging like a full moon over the hill of the future to tantalise and weaken her. No hope for a new year made the present drab and tasteless to her. This day she flourished, breathed, felt the heat, and waited for Stan. And with him, she lived.

Time before him was vague and dim. If David mentioned people she had met in the past, she tried to remember them, conciliating him. A string of talking puppets, hollow, identical, assembled for her, and one of them was herself. There was nothing she wished to remember. It was better left grey and blurred.

She thought if she could feel in Stan the counterpart of her own content with the present, she would be entirely happy and free from strain. What could he need or want? He was not ambitious—except for money. But was that true? She wondered. That she was, herself, a fulfilled ambition to Stan, worn by him as another man might wear a knighthood, she did not understand. But it seemed evident to her that, generally speaking,

133

he was not. They never discussed the future or made plans. There seemed no necessity. It was obvious that children would not have fitted into their life. Why had she thought it a good idea?

So there are to be no children. All right. But why keep saying it? she asked with a kind of bitter irritation. I understood the first time. I'm never to have Stan's child.

'Hi, darling!' Stan leaned over her. 'Were you asleep? Don't blame you.' He flopped heavily into a chair, threw his hat off and wiped his face with a handkerchief. 'I've been out at that confounded factory all day with Ron. It was cruel. It was like an oven.'

'How is everything going?'

'Oh fine, fine. We'll soon have them on the market.'

'What are they working on now?'

He grinned. 'You don't really want to know that, honey. If I told you, you still wouldn't know. All you have to do is take the pretty things they let me buy for you. Now!' He took off his coat and tie and stood up to haul his shirt over his head. 'I'm off to have a shower.' He collected his clothes under one arm and started to go. 'Oh, by the way,' he said casually, 'talking of pretty things, I've got something in here you might like.'

Esther went in, her hands loosely clasped in front of her.

'What is it?'

'On the table.'

One transparent cellophane box held a spray of gardenias, and a small white leather case, satin-lined, displayed when opened a magnificent pair of diamond pendant earrings.

At last she said, 'They're beautiful, Stan!'

He frowned at the earrings disdainfully. 'Think so?' Then he grinned. 'Not bad, are they? Why shouldn't you have them, pet? We're doing well.' They held each other.

Later that night, when they sat at a small table at Zito's nightclub, his eyes turned again and again to the shimmering stones that swung against Esther's neck whenever she moved her head. Stan leaned back so that he could see her from a distance. He looped one arm over the top of his chair. He explored his teeth ruminatively with his tongue. What could he compare her to, he wondered critically. Irrelevantly, it struck him as a pity that she preferred champagne to whisky. He felt better than this on whisky. Still—he went back to his original problem—what could he compare her to? Nothing, he decided, swinging round to the table with a thump; she was on her own. Just on her own.

He glanced coldly at the women sitting nearest him. One, whose skin was the colour of cinnamon, whose dress was gold, was caught at the crisis of a long and trying joke. She shook her yellow head and laughed with relief, longer than was necessary.

Mouth like a shark, Stan condemned her disgustedly.

He looked next at a young girl whose red-gold hair gleamed in the artificial light. The colour appalled him; her animation and her youth made him turn away.

His pride and satisfaction fell to pieces. All young things reminded him of age. He should have stayed at the top of the tree forever. It wasn't in the bargain, he hadn't understood, that he would get old, that he would ever be more than twenty-five or so. The lost years, the best years, were behind him now, untouchable, used up, the damage done. And here he was, doing all right, but still not what he should have been, and not going to have another chance—ever. Just getting older and older while crowds of redheaded girls...

'I want to get out of here. Let's go home,' he said to Esther. 'It's nearly half-past one.'

In the car she said, 'I like champagne.' She began to hum one of the tunes they had danced to. 'I like dancing with you, Stan. You're so...' And then she remembered that there was something she had to guard against, keep out of her mind, and she wondered what it was. She sat motionless, staring with unfocused eyes at the road ahead.

'Yeah, it was great,' Stan declared with an effort. 'Great.' He repeated the last word as he often did to show that he was a man of strong opinions.

'This was a kind of going-away party, tonight,' he said suddenly, the words and the idea coming together. 'Have to leave you next week, pet. Gotta go to Melbourne to see about some business. I'd take you along,' he said, punching the car horn viciously with the side of his clenched fist, 'only I'll be on the move all the time. It'd be no fun by yourself in a hotel room. You're better at home.' He caught at her hand and squeezed it for a moment.

'Don't leave me,' she said in a low voice.

'I told you why,' he said patiently. 'You'll be fine. It'll only be for a week.'

And whether it was because Esther had sounded heartsick at the news, or because he had proved to himself that he had some control over his life, Stan felt the warmth of rising confidence.

Holding her mouth carefully open, Vi swept the small brush, heavy with red polish, along her nail and then popped it neatly back into the bottle. She removed a thin line of polish from the tip of her nail with an orange-stick and relaxed.

'Thank God!' Stan said irritably. 'I hate the smell of that stuff.'

They sat in Vi's bedroom, a sunny pale-blue room with flower prints on the walls and a pink rug on the floor. A hot breeze billowed the gauzy curtains out over Stan's head; peevishly he grabbed at them and pushed them back.

Seeing his mood, Vi glanced thoughtfully at her sticky nails, and blew a token breath to dry them.

Her lips still pursed, she turned again to regard Stan, who, elbows on knees, eyes on carpet, was smoking a cigarette with ferocious attention.

'I forgot to tell you Eck was asking for you last night,' she began mildly, but seeing the blank hostility in his eyes as he raised his head, she said abruptly, 'Listen, Stan. If you've changed that master mind of yours about this trip you'd better say so. Don't think I've taken a week off to go to Melbourne so that you can have me for an audience for one of your famous moods, pal, because you're wrong!'

She stared at him indignantly, her small hands still raised, fingers outspread to protect her nails. It was like a childish gesture of protest.

The hardness left Stan's eyes. 'Cute lid you've got,' he said, waving at her hat.

Vi's stiff black lashes rose as she rolled her eyes up in an effort to see it. 'What's wrong with it? It was damn dear.'

They grinned at each other. Stan stood up and stretched his arms. 'Time that taxi was here.'

'I'll just make sure all the windows are closed.'

He watched Vi as she went through to the other room with short quick steps. Screwing his face up, he massaged his neck for a moment and wished that he was twenty. He sighed, remembering the good feeling of being young and being with men. He remembered the days spent swopping yarns and studying form, hanging round the courses, waiting for the piece of luck that would make their fortunes. Females came and went in those days: a man had the sense not to get involved. Well, you couldn't say Vi came and went—but she was different. She was a real good-looker and she'd had a head full of sense even then: she could sum up a horse or a drink or a deal. Still, women were all alike. They always meant trouble, he reflected morosely. No peace, no good times. Aw hell, he could do with a real binge. It'd cheer a fellow up.

'What are you mumbling about?' Vi looked into the room and he stared at her foolishly. 'Back in a jiff.' She was off again without waiting for an answer.

'God, I've worked this week to get away,' he said aloud, as if she were there. He had a vision of himself at the wheel of the car, racing from the factory to the houses of his salesmen and agents, from the docks to the factory, and from there, the tedious trail around the suburbs to the homes of the women who assembled his novelty lines. A fellow must be off his rocker, he grumbled. But in truth, he was soothed by the memory of business. Unconsciously he wiped his mouth with the palm of his hand to hide the smile that had appeared there.

The help he had received from Jim and Toddy after they went over to the States was incalculable, but he could be independent of them now if he chose; he had found his own contacts. But he'd stick to them, of course; Stan Peterson would never let his old pals down. It hadn't all been easy sailing: he'd run risks, but that was in the game, a bit of danger was fun to anyone worth his salt. And a few notes to the right man at the right time kept everything sweet. The work and the worry and the final reward—he enjoyed every move.

'Take your filthy shoes off my bed!'

He stood up and laughed in his humourless way while Vi inspected the filmy blue covers which had been ordered especially to match the curtains. 'Just as well,' she said. 'Don't do that again.'

She looked at him provocatively, standing with her weight on one leg, the other thrust forward, one hand on her hip. It was a pose she liked, but she dropped it a moment later to say, 'All I want to know is—do you want me to come with you or not?'

'Strike a bloody light! What do you want me to do? Go down on my ruddy knees? Haven't I said so?'

'Yes, but you meant it then.' She looked at him, half angry, half doubtful.

'Well, for crying out loud, what's the matter with you? Of course, I meant it,' he said, exasperated.

'Okay, honey,' she smiled. 'Keep calm. Oh! There's the door! The taxi! Where's my bag? Where's my gloves? Answer the door, will you, love? Yours'll be along in a minute, won't he? All this business—going in two taxis. No one'd see us if we went together. I could sit on the floor. So long. See you at the airport. And Stan!' she

140

called as she banged the door. 'Don't forget to close that window. There's going to be a storm.'

'Women!' he exclaimed. But by the time he ran downstairs to catch his taxi he was whistling.

CHAPTER FOURTEEN

How did it start? How did it ever start, and why? Esther answered her question with another. Because Stan wanted to quarrel was the only answer, and she knew it.

Four times in the three weeks that had passed since his return from Melbourne he had come home at night flushed with whisky, wearing an attitude of such truculence that it seemed to precede him into the flat. In sullen brooding silence he ate his dinner, half turned from the table, sprawled in his chair, cramming food into his mouth and pulling exaggerated faces of distaste as he chewed, looking every moment as though he might spit it out, or be sick.

Settling back in an armchair with another drink, he unrolled a newspaper, or took some sheets of paper and covered them with pencilled hieroglyphics referring to the factory output. Supposedly occupied, he covertly watched Esther as she cleared the table and washed the dishes in the kitchen with nervous haste. She knew he watched her and he knew she knew. His lips curled with malicious satisfaction that he succeeded in stripping her of her repose. He felt his power swell within him, and he loved it as a pregnant woman loves her unborn child.

Each night, as tonight, Esther returned to the room with a piece of sewing, or a magazine, or letters that she should write, to keep the appearance of normality in her small routine; at the same time she held herself ready to do whatever might pacify him, to check a movement or word that seemed to displease. But she underrated him in thinking that her actions only were on trial, while her existence, and her family's, and the joint and separate pasts of each of them were undeniable facts.

The way she looks at me! he thought, as he stared glassy-eyed at the paper. She appeared to his drunken mind as something loathsome beyond description, something to be tormented and squashed.

His voice came at her suddenly and she went rigid at the hate in it. Coherent thought failed in the wake of such venom, leaving her stranded in total darkness, like someone in a house where lightning has cut the current. Instinct alone, called up by alarm, caused her hand to rise and fall over her sewing and kept her eyes on the shining needle. It mercifully dulled her hearing and slowed her breathing, so that for long stretches of time, while the voice sneered and cross-examined, she was barely half alive.

The paper had fallen from his hand, and he lay back in his chair, hands in pockets, talking, talking. 'God!' he interrupted himself to exclaim every now and then. Looking at Esther in a long cold silence, 'Jesus!' he said.

'And this thing thinks she's better than Mr Stan Peterson, better than Mr Peterson, does she? She thinks she can tell him what to do, does she?'

He snorted and poured out another drink. 'Well, she's bloody well wrong!' he said after another long, deliberate pause. 'And her great gentlemen brothers! Huh! All they're good for's sittin' on their great fat behinds! The al-bloody-mighty Prescotts.'

In a sudden paroxysm of rage he looked round for something to smash, and with a shout of satisfaction lifted his foot and kicked a tall vase of fine blue china from the table near his chair. It cracked as his foot touched it, and shattered as it bounced sharply against the wall.

Esther cried out involuntarily.

'Yeah!' he said. 'That's what I think of their presents. Silly damn useless thing.'

She started to fold her sewing with the precise movements of someone who is fighting for control. Stan jerked up in his chair, watching her suspiciously. He had been waiting for some sign of feeling from her; the night would have been tasteless without it.

144

'Where d'ya think you're goin'?' he smiled.

Esther kept stacking her cottons in the basket. 'To bed.'

'Huh! Like hell y'are. You'll go when I'm good and ready. When Mr Stan Peterson says so. You stay where y'are!' He poured another drink and mumbled to himself, keeping his eyes fixed on her. 'Uh-uh!' He half rose, warningly, and she said, 'All right. I'll stay.'

Occasionally Stan pretended that he was going over to force an answer to his rhetorical questions, but his legs were tired, and his ideas of what he might do when he reached her unformed, so he relapsed, each time, into his chair with a show of forbearance.

No sign that he remembered the sober shame of other mornings showed on his bloated face, or disturbed the confident twist on his mouth. But gradually, as the hours moved by, his periods of brooding became longer, and his voice grew more thick and slurred. Finally, after many false starts, when the finger had ceased to wag, and the hand to find the bottle and glass, he drew himself from the chair with agonising slowness, and, turning on Esther one last contemptuous stare in lieu of the rebuke he could not frame, lurched from the room and banged the door behind him.

Esther did not move, but gradually, as the tension uncoiled within her, she let her weight fall on the back of the sofa, and lay as if pinned there until she heard the bedroom door slam.

'Oh, God! Oh, God!' She shaped the words with her lips, silently, as if by even so slight a movement to prove her reality to herself; feeling, too, dimly, that the woman who could move and think must somehow comfort the woman who had been abused and could do neither. But a sense of cosmic loneliness, and of her own incapacity, swept over her chillily.

She would not remember. Her eyes opened wide with hostility at the thought. She would not remember.

At last, with a surge of energy that came from nowhere, she got up and moved about the room, gathering the broken china with animal caution lest she should disturb Stan, who, two rooms away, slept and snored. Turning off the white wall lamps then, she lay down on the sofa, fully dressed.

Moonlight had displaced air in the small low-ceilinged room, for although the windows and the balcony door were open wide, the wavering breeze could not force the silvery walls. The room was alight with subtle colour. Esther felt exposed by the light and stifled by the warmth. She hated the calm beauty of the summer night that bloomed indifferent to all human feeling.

What did I do? What did I do to change him? Her memory scurried frantically to find the reason, offering up trivialities of every kind as it dredged, but nothing that she could accept, nothing that she could reject, with certainty, as the cause. I've seemed to criticise.

Her thoughts spun round, questioning, unchanging: only the pain they produced expanded. Yet it was self-defensive, less sharp than the memories it held off. She drew her legs up and bent her head over her knees, centring herself in the smallest space possible, drawing help from the warmth of her own body.

David poked around in his pipe before he looked at Clem. Esther and Stan, Hector and Angela, had gone, and Marion was upstairs. Another family gathering was over. 'Well, what do you think?'

Clem went over to lock the French windows. 'Tonight? Everything was all right, wasn't it? I thought it went off rather better than usual, in fact.'

'What about Esther?'

'Yes...I know what you mean.' He frowned as he came back and straddled the chair opposite his brother. 'She seemed a bit unlike herself—especially with Stan.'

'I thought so, too,' David said heavily. 'And I suppose the others noticed.'

Clem grasped the back of the chair. 'There was something ingratiating about the way she behaved to him—and yet, when you think of it, it's an incredible word to apply to her. It was probably nothing. Perhaps she was only trying to keep him in a good humour for our benefit.'

David looked concerned. 'I shouldn't like to think she had to make such efforts to keep his temper even.'

'We've no reason to believe he's bad-tempered or anything else—there was nothing wrong with him tonight. We simply don't know the fellow, and as long as he can help it, we won't. And,' he said, looking at his watch, 'if it comes to that—how well do we know Esther?...Well, I'm going up now, David.' He levered himself out of the chair.

His brother took no notice. 'I don't know what I ought to do.'

'There's nothing you can do,' Clem said, 'short of asking her straight out if everything's under control. I don't see how you can do that without immediately letting her know that the discussions she must suspect we have about them do take place. As they do. But I think it would be a pity if she knew.'

David abandoned his pipe with a sigh. 'You're right, of course, but your advice is a bit late. I did try to talk to her tonight—to ask her.'

Raising his eyebrows in surprise, trying to conceal his disapproval, Clem asked, 'How did you get on?'

'Upset her. She didn't like it. I had to pass it off.'

'Yes. We're probably making too much of the whole thing...even Hector and Angela have an occasional row, you know.'

David looked disbelieving. 'You think it was something like that?'

'I don't know. She's not an adolescent. She can manage her husband without our help. She managed to get along before she was married without any interference from us. Forget it! Leave them in peace.'

There was a silence which was broken at length by David asking, 'Where did you say you left Winter's papers? I want to look at them before I go to bed.'

'On your desk in the study.'

Clem strolled around with his hands in his pockets for a while, his lips pursed as if he were whistling. He took a cheese straw from a dish that had been accidentally left behind and considered it very thoroughly before he finally ate it.

Quite suddenly, but some time after the wish first came to him, Stan's drinking bout ended. The delay between decision and consummation was a necessary sop to dignity, as he saw it.

As he drove from house to house, collecting completed work, delivering loose material, he spent long hours reviewing his case. He would justify his outburst and prove that as the reasons for it still existed, so he should continue in the same way. But contrariwise, and sometimes in the same half-hour, he was forced to defend the course he was going to adopt, and prove that all right lay on its side. Undoubtedly right in all his actions, past, present and future, he showed himself to be.

It was right to stop when a man had a hangover every day, and his stomach felt crook, and he couldn't keep track of the boys. But then, it had been right to start when a man couldn't visit an old friend like Vi without feeling guilty, when he had the thousands and the wife he'd always wanted, and hardly cared.

Was it Est's fault? No, he wouldn't exactly say that. All he was saying was that he wasn't in the wrong.

He had found, though he did not admit it, that baiting someone with pride was work he could take pleasure in. And when, at the same time, he regarded that pride as a kind of Holy Grail, so much the better. That was commando stuff of a high order for any man's spirit. But when the pride had been killed, or at any rate battered unconscious, then it was time to stop and wonder. To live with the grey figure of humility was retribution enough. His teeth were on edge when faced with Esther's awful anxiety. His old fear that he had been tricked into marrying the wrong woman reappeared. She was a fake, he thought, and he had been taken.

But gradually the spurious worked-up hate and indignation died away and a new kind of dread came to life. He thought he had indeed destroyed the nameless quality that meant Esther to him—the cool stillness, the apparent certainty of voice and action, the sympathy and passion.

The flow of justifications ceased, for he dimly comprehended that he had damaged the fabric of life. Rather, he had been misused by the gods.

CHAPTER FIFTEEN

For five days the city had wilted under a hard sky, sweltering in a temperature that stayed fixed in the middle nineties. Even at night there was no relief from the heat. Pyjamas and nighties stuck clammily to damp skin. Half-clad, self-pitying figures rose, exasperated by insomnia, to stumble through darkened rooms in search of a cooler plot than their bed, hoping that, all accidentally, they might waken any gross sleeper the house contained.

Cold water ran hot from the taps, and the roads turned to tar. Doors and windows slid to and fro, pulled open by pro-air enthusiasts, and slammed by those who were anti-heat, and therefore, anti-air.

On Saturday, free from work, the dehydrated citizens fled to the beaches and pools to immerse themselves in as large a body of cold water as they could find; dreaming, too, that there on the shore they might suddenly lift their faces to the cooling wash of an ocean breeze, a forerunner of cool weather.

Laura Maitland sat on a folded towel, her back against the cement wall that enclosed the shingle, her face in the shade of a striped beach umbrella. Pretty, tanned girls and tall brown men strode to and fro along the beach. Sometimes she was splashed by the water that dripped from skin and hair; sometimes a flapping towel sent sand in showers round her. She closed her eyes and bore it. She opened them and looked around.

As they are on beaches everywhere, people were scattered about like narrow dark rocks, motionless, silent, sun-worshipping. They aggravated Laura.

I'm absolutely limp, she thought. This place is like a blast furnace. She removed her sunglasses and wiped her face.

'Will you keep an eye on her, dear, while I have a swim?' Bill appeared round the side of the umbrella and dumped Anabel in the sand at Laura's feet. 'I've given her a long play in the water. She should be a good girl now,' he said, turning from one to the other.

With a placating smile to Laura he went off to the diving boards, and in spite of her vexation she could not resist the thrill of pleasure that the sight of his legs gave her as he walked away. 'For an old married man of thirty-six, you've got the best legs at the pool, angel,' she would say to him when he came back. She rehearsed it, and her face softened indulgently.

Anabel, sitting outside the radius of shade cast by the umbrella, had begun to dig with her painted spade. Gazing at her small serious face, with its beautiful forehead and eyes, Laura's smile deepened, and momentarily she forgot her discomfort while her eyes caressed the slender neck that was exposed by the looping up of the long brown hair.

As they came down the steps, Esther said, 'Oh, Stan! There's Laura!'

They stood looking for a vacant space to leave their towels and sandals.

'Maybe she won't see us in the crowd.'

'Hello,' Laura called in a jolly voice.

Esther smiled. 'She's waving. We'll have to go over for a minute.'

'Wouldn't you know it!' Stan said.

Their feet sank in the dry, burning shingle as they made their way up the slope towards her.

Laura admitted that there was a certain pre-bathing elegance about the two of them: the spare brown bodies, the severe black costumes, the dark glasses and the combed hair. Stan's got good legs, too, she thought.

'Like us, you've come for a breeze,' she said ironically when they reached her. 'Isn't it ghastly?'

And they discussed the various, hopeless methods of keeping cool. When Bill came up, he and Stan stood a little apart from the women talking in confidential tones about a temporary shortage of bottled beer.

Lightly, Laura said to Esther, 'You haven't been in to see me for ages?'

'I know. I was not feeling well for a week or so, and I rested as much as I could.' She felt the sympathetic eyes go over her face.

'And now?' Laura prompted. 'I think you're looking marvellous, to tell the truth.'

'I feel really well again.'

They smiled at one another with their mouths as they fenced.

'I'd have been up a dozen times to see what was wrong, but it isn't easy when you have a poppet like this one.' Anabel looked round at her tone. 'And then, I like to think that we're friends and that you'd let me know if I could help in any way.'

Faintly annoyed by Laura's probing, Esther said with the cool voice and face she turned to everyone but Stan, 'You're very kind, Laura,' and left it at that.

Laura thought: I'll get somewhere with her yet. Esther pushed her hair under the bathing cap, while Stan stood watching her with proprietorial pride. 'How about this swim?' he said.

The water was cold against hot skin, and they splashed gingerly through the shallows, a thrill of apprehension sharpening as the cold tide climbed their legs. Stan went under first, and came up laughing, dashing his hair back and blinking the salt water away. Esther dived and swam for a distance under water, keeping her eyes open. When she surfaced, gasping and exhilarated, she joined Stan, and together they swam out to the narrow ledge that formed a promenade around the pool. Heavy with water, they hauled themselves up. The heat struck them, but for the moment it was almost pleasant. Esther dangled her feet in the water and gazed around.

In front lay the pool, dark blue, thrashed to foam by hundreds of arms and legs. Strong swimmers churned across its width and divers struck its surface and disappeared. Boys stood on their hands on the sea bed and waved their legs in the air.

Only the faintest echo penetrated the tight white rubber cap so that the unheard cry from the smiling mouth, the soundless shouts, the vivacity and brightness under the shining sky, gave her a curious sense of being an invisible spectator at some eternal pageant. A sheet of glass or a world of time separated her from the players.

Stan's eyes were closed. She rubbed her legs with her hands; they were warm and dry again; fine salt moved under her fingers. Turning, she looked at the harbour behind her. Small white-sailed boats stood motionless in the hot air while a fast green ferry moved down on them, its outside upper deck crammed with faces and waving arms.

Esther looked away; she leaned her head on the railing and closed her eyes, but the light streamed through her lids. She sighed with satisfaction.

In dreams, at times, emotions have a deeper pulse, come from a purer stream, and consequently differ in degree from conscious feeling. To a similar degree Esther's love for Stan had been extended by unhappiness and comprehension of its cause.

Summoned by Laura's curiosity of a few minutes before, the scene played out again in front of her. She could hear Stan's hopeless voice, see the pattern made by his story.

'I don't like the way I am, but it's too late—I can't help it,' he had said, struggling, for once in his life, to reach some truth, some understanding of himself.

Esther had listened in silence, shocked by the inarticulate complexity of his defence. That there was no single reason to account for his behaviour of the past weeks at first terrified her. That there were half reasons by the score taught her that her previous knowledge of him had been superficial.

She opened her eyes and splashed her legs vigorously, dismissing her thoughts.

Her sudden movement disturbed Stan, and he stretched and yawned noisily. 'How are you, honey?' he asked.

'All right. How are you?' she smiled.

'Fine...Do you know you splashed me just then?

Look!' He pointed to some drops of water on his chest. 'Maybe I should push you in for that.'

'I hate to go in feet first.'

'Well, I'll let you off this time because there just happens to be something about you I like. So you're lucky!'

They smiled at each other and stayed there talking for a few minutes longer, trying to decide on their afternoon's entertainment.

'Are you *sure* you'd like to go to the races?' Stan said. 'I'd be just as pleased to do something else...Palm Beach.'

'No, no, the races. You'd like it best and I've got a new hat. Besides, I like the races.'

They stood for a moment before diving in again.

'Isn't that young Rachel over there? Look! Just coming out of the water,' Stan said. 'Green costume.'

'Oh yes. She seems to be going up to Laura. That's Signor Roberto with her, I think.'

'Signor!'

Luigi and Rachel walked along the beach.

'Do you mind?' she asked, as she waved back to Laura.

'I look forward to it,' said Luigi.

Rachel glanced at him and felt still with happiness.

'What is it I must remember about Mrs Maitland?' he asked.

Rachel smiled vaguely. 'Oh, just that she's as nice

157

as she pretends to be. In a way,' she added, 'she under-estimates herself.'

Listening to Laura, Luigi thought it was prob-ably a fair statement. Sitting on the shingle beside her, they were her guests—the beach belonged to her. She was the hostess whose duty it was to radiate, and she did, giving a stimulus and pleasure that were out of all proportion to anything that was said or done. They all enjoyed themselves.

Rachel looked from one to the other, thankful that Laura had not decided to tackle Luigi about Abyssinia, hoping that he would not be over-charmed, chiding herself for this when she caught his eye.

'Well, Miss Demster.' Laura turned to her suddenly. 'What's this I hear about you? Your aunt tells me that when you're not out at night with this young man, you're busy studying. Are you responsible for this?' she asked Luigi.

'Indirectly,' he said, turning to look at Rachel. 'I may have acted as catalyst.'

'Catalyst?' Rachel blinked, baffled.

'Ah!' Laura exclaimed, and laughed while she tried to guess his meaning. Failing, she said flatly, 'Well, it wouldn't do for me! I think you're both very foolish. You should dance and go to parties and leave all the studying to the clever ones.'

Luigi smiled and said, 'You are right, in a way, of course, but we...'

'Well, I think I can say that I'm a few years older than either you,' Laura said cheerfully in explanation.

Just then Bill came back with Anabel, who had been in the water again. She cried out with excitement when she saw Rachel with her mother and, hugging and tugging, did her best to commandeer Rachel's notice. Quite soon the two were engaged on a castle, and the others watched and smiled, agreeing wordlessly that it was, indeed, a very pretty picture.

Glancing at Luigi, Laura conceded that, for an Italian, and in the quiet way she rather liked, he was charming. And he had a nice face, and spoke English well.

'Pauline and Bob aren't coming down today, Rae?' Bill asked.

'No, poor things, they're visiting. They're going away for a holiday soon, though. Tasmania—for a month. There you are, sweetie,' she said to Anabel. 'Isn't that a lovely castle?'

'You'll be alone in the flat?' Laura asked.

Looking up from her tunnelling, Rachel said, 'Yes, but I don't mind that.'

'Of course you don't. Still, you must come and have some meals with us, mustn't she, Ani-Anabel?'

The Petersons passed on their way home and stopped briefly to talk. When they had gone, Laura said, 'We must move in a moment, too, or our child will be sunburnt—not to mention her mother!'

159

Extremely reluctant, Anabel had her sandals buckled on and her red-and-white checked sunbonnet tied. She had to say goodbye to her castle with its cool, damp tunnel where Rae's hand had come through to catch hers. Just when they had been starting to dig something called a moat she was taken away, and Rae was left sitting there with the castle on one side and that man on the other.

'Goodbye, darling.' Laura patted Rachel on the head, her voice rich. Youth—Rachel in love. Life was endlessly interesting.

CHAPTER SIXTEEN

Summer ran through its repertoire. It brought fresh sunny days, disastrous rains and thunderstorms, heat that lasted for weeks, heat that lasted for a day and bowed at sunset to the onslaught of a 'southerly buster'.

The country drought contrived to ruin a few small farmers, but, curiously, left those who counted thousands by hundreds no poorer. While world affairs trod the same serious circle, small boys fought over precedence at drinking bubblers in burnt-up parks. Freckled, shaggy and gap-toothed, they whooped and racketed at every beach and pool for miles around the city, escaping from school whenever they could.

The daily journey to shop and office and factory went on although brains lazed and ambition died. The air-conditioned oases of restaurant and cinema made life bearable for those who had leisure, and there were few who lacked a moderate share.

In florists' windows exotic flowers hung in waxy beauty, scented and cooled a space of air outside the shops in a subtle form of advertising that compelled attention from the passerby. And in the streets, women in big straw hats that cast warm patterns of light and shade on skin, walked in thin high shoes, their dresses circling in the breeze.

Moist sea-winds dimmed brasses from the East. Housewives polished the bloom from their furniture, and shop windows were rubbed with soft cloths, but still the sea-mist settled and clouded the shine. It salted the lips and straightened the hair while it gladdened the spirits.

Earnest and snubbed, the old-young New Australians went unsmiling through the streets, despising and fearing the lotus-eaters among whom they now lived, despised and feared by them.

'They do not know life. They do not know what life is,' they told each other, and envy took its place beside contempt. They bent over their work with determination and ignored the heat and the happy laughter outside. But everyone else knew that summer had no end.

At this time Stan had worked out a new routine that involved leaving home early in the morning so that he could return correspondingly earlier and spend more time with Esther. Even so, his programmes of orders, collections and deliveries, and the visits to the factory occupied him until the afternoon. He counted on being in by three o'clock. Then came the ritualistic greetings that had begun after the reconciliation and not yet petered out, and the first drink of the day, together, drunk with the same air of consciousness.

A sense of grace, a surprised sense of the pleasure of living, had appeared in Stan since he and Esther had come together again. He valued small things, and content, and relaxation: he seemed to have stumbled on a dimension of life that had previously been outside his range. Whether this was brought on by relief, or by some other cause, he did not try to discover. He saw it as a reward for good behaviour, a compensation for growing old. There was about this settled state a feeling of permanence and reliability which was something entirely new.

'This is living!' He said it often as he stretched out beside Esther on the balcony. 'It takes a man a long time to wake up to himself, but when he does...' And they would smile at each other.

Every morning after Stan had gone, Esther tidied and dusted and planned dinner. Sometimes then she put on a bathing costume and lay in the sun, but just as often she met Laura and they shopped together, smartly dressed and prosperous—Laura sensitively aware of the life in the crowded streets;

Esther apparently interested, actually dreamy and inattentive, living for the afternoon.

Guessing this, Laura taxed her with it one day, saying, 'No one could adore her husband more than I do Bill, but when he isn't with me (though God knows I wish he always were) I make the best of it and enjoy myself. That way I have things to tell when he comes home at night and I'm not leaving all the entertaining to him.'

'You're very sensible, Laura,' Esther said, and Laura, incredulous and indignant, thought: Really, I believe the woman's shy about discussing her blessed Stan.

It was by no means the first time she had been forced to this conclusion, but its ultimate recognition never ceased to frustrate her.

Whichever way you looked at it, Esther was a disappointment. She would say goodbye and go upstairs when the shopping was done, so charming, so polite, but not caring that she went. Cold-natured. Rather hard.

Yet even as she made this judgement Laura denied it, for she was finding, as she knew her better, much that was warm and endearing in Esther's nature. They laughed together a lot.

Esther had a youthful self-mocking quality which showed itself when, eyebrows an inverted V of incredulity, she would tell some story against herself—of absent-mindedness, of misplaced or misinterpreted sensibility—not trying to make an impression but being amusing, being herself. So that, even while Laura asked herself with cold scientific interest what made Esther tick, some side of her personality found Esther's light and undemanding manner infinitely refreshing.

But here you were; again today she had gone off as soon as they reached home, saying, no, thank you, but she wouldn't stay to share Laura's lunch, for she had to organise herself for the dinner engagement that she and Stan had tonight with Clem and his girl friend, Erica.

The organisation, sounding so weighty, consisted of nothing more difficult than confirming an already-taken decision to wear the short white evening dress. And this was done almost before she had gone five steps from Laura's door.

After that, a telephone call to Marion, one from Clem, watering the trail of ivy that fell down the white wall opposite the windows, three cigarettes, and a solitary lunch filled in the time until Stan came home.

And then, after having so much time, they stayed out on the balcony talking until they had to rush to shower and dress. At least, Esther dressed swiftly, but Stan, who had been in high spirits all afternoon, moved in a slow preoccupied haze between bathroom and bedroom, his hands apparently working without co-operation or assistance from his mind.

Noticing, Esther said nothing. He would be ready soon, and if they were a little late it would be no calamity. She stepped into her dress and lifted it carefully.

Stan stood watching her. He said suddenly, 'Est...'

'What?...Oh, would you help with this zip, please, pet?...That's it.' She sat down at the dressing table and Stan stood behind her, watching her hands as if hypnotised while they found the mascara and started to apply it. 'What were you going to say, darling?'

He put his hands in his pockets and walked away, coughing slightly. 'I was wondering today—well, I've been thinking about it for a while now—I've been thinking that you might like it if we set up house in a big way. You know—here somewhere or on the north shore. Nice garden and so on. What do you think?'

She looked at him, surprised. 'Buy a house, Stan?'

'Well, you know, this place is all right for a while, but look at this room—the size of it—and so damn stuffy in this weather. You should have a place where you could ask people over for dinner. Nice garden and so on. Good furniture. You'd know what to get.' He appealed to her and she murmured, 'Yes, yes. We might like that,' while she tried to see behind his restless eyes to the point he obviously had not reached. They stared at one another in silence for a moment, trying to communicate without words, but at last Stan jerked away and laughed, shame-faced.

'Well—maybe I'm off my rocker—but I was just wondering what you'd think about us having a kid? I don't know why, but it just struck me it might be a good idea.' His eyes were all over the room, and he spoke very fast, not giving her a chance to interrupt. 'We get on

166

fine without one—maybe it's a lousy idea, I don't know.'
He gave an almost theatrical shrug of indifference. A
moment later he turned excited eyes on Esther and she
was caught.

A pang of extraordinary desolation swept over her
heart and spread to every nerve of her body. It ached in
the palms of her hands.

'I can't. I saw a doctor months ago and he said it isn't
possible.' She spoke in a voice so dry and lifeless that Stan
would not have understood if he had not read her lips.

With dead eyes she surveyed the blankness on his
face as he tried to take it in; she caught blindly at his
hand. 'Oh, darling…I can't bear it. I can't bear to disap-
point you like this. I'm so sorry.'

He put a hand on her head, smoothed her hair.
'Sorry?' he echoed vaguely. 'Be sensible, Est.' He kept
stroking her hair. 'You went to see a doctor? Why didn't
you tell me?…Well…' He could think of nothing more
to say, and, being conditioned to close his mouth over
a cigarette on such occasions, he lifted a packet from
the dressing table, shook two into his hand, lit them
with enormous concentration, and gave one to Esther.

She held it and looked at him mutely, silently entreat-
ing another word, but Stan strolled about the room,
elaborately casual, as if he were outdoors, on holiday.

'Oh, yes,' he said, as if he had remembered
something he must do, and, humming tunelessly, he
transferred wallets, papers, keys, pen and samples of

plastic from the pockets of the suit he had been wearing to his dinner suit. Then, noticing what he had done, he took them all out again.

'Stan.'

He swung round and gave a forced laugh when he saw that he had been observed. 'Now look here,' he began on a note of extreme reason, groping unwillingly for words. 'Just because I…well…' He took a deep breath and threw his arms about. 'Just because I have some mad idea there's no need for you to…' As Esther turned slowly away he broke off, and gazed stupidly at the narrow shoulders left bare by the tight white dress, gazed at the diamond earrings, the dark hair.

The thin bleating tinkle of the alarm clock broke the silence. Small reverberations of shock sent pulsing heat over Esther's skin.

'Hell!' said Stan.

Esther pressed the black knob on the clock and the bell was quiet. 'I must have wound it up,' she said, letting her hands fall heavily to her lap.

'Quarter to eight! We're going to be late! A fine time I pick to talk about a thing like this. Are we nearly ready?' He looked at her busily, pretending nothing was wrong.

'I don't know. I can't think.'

He drew her to her feet. 'Now look,' he said with rough kindliness, 'you've got to forget all about this and cheer up. Forget it.' He held her and waited. 'Will you do what I tell you?'

Her nerves cried out for the relief of honest words, for—not a scene that would leave her comforted and Stan deprived, but—*something* more than had been said.

Now, however, he was regarding her with a baffling insincerity that made them less than strangers. He would neither acknowledge nor revile.

She frowned, drew breath to speak, but shook her head instead, and giving up, leaned against him.

It was then, unpremeditated, that she asked, 'Could we adopt a child, Stan? Would you? Would you hate to?' And she moved back to study his face.

'Adopt?' His hands slipped from her shoulders. 'I never thought about it.' There was a pause and each could feel a lightening, a rising hope. '*Could* we?...I don't see why not, though.'

'The doctor said we should think about it, but of course, I...'

'What do you think yourself, Est? Can you see us with a family in a couple of weeks?' He was ablaze with enthusiasm.

She looked at him.

'A boy and a girl?' he said. 'Could we get two at once? Or should we start with one? Or what?'

Esther, lacking Stan's easeful volatility, felt the need to sit down. He repeated a question and she cried, 'Oh, I don't know!' She gazed blankly at the floor, down the hall, up at Stan.

'I wasn't prepared for this,' she said, with the youthfulness of utter confusion, and Stan laughed. The welling tension broke and he roared with laughter; he sat down beside her on the bed and laughed until his eyes watered; he put a hand on her knee, heavily, to support himself, to join himself to her in this moment of supreme amusement.

An unwilling smile, caught from Stan, half pity, half hysteria, came to her reluctant mouth. At last Stan wiped his eyes.

Esther said, 'But it wouldn't be the same, would it? You'd feel—you must feel—it's natural that you should...' He tried to stop her but she warded him off with upraised arms. 'After I saw the doctor I hoped I'd never have to tell you. You'd never said...we'd never planned...but I didn't really feel so very miserable about it. I suppose I'm not maternal—not like Laura—I'm selfish...I might even have been jealous. Oh!' she jerked around on the bed with a wail, 'but that's not true either. I did care about it. You must know that I did. How could I not?' Leaning away from him, against the back of the bed, she pressed her lips together and Stan stroked her neck with his big soft hand.

After a few minutes he heaved himself up from the bed and bent over her. 'Now!' he said decisively. 'We're going to have one drink each and then we're going to scram. We'll talk about all this in the car, or later, or sometime soon, and you're going to have a good time tonight and so am I. Do you hear me?' He spoke to her in the firm hypnotic tone of one who would have obedience, and, struck by it, and by the rare gentleness in it, she opened her eyes and looked at him. They exchanged a smile that had in it everything of themselves.

Stan marched off and Esther sat still for a moment, her hands clasped, looking through the empty door where he had gone.

When he came back from the kitchen he put the glasses down and stared anxiously in the wardrobe mirror. 'Thirty-four and forty-one, Est. Are we too old?' he asked, examining his skin, smoothing his hair.

Esther went slowly up to him. 'No!' she said in a tone sufficiently eloquent to force a vain, relieved grin to his face. 'I wondered, that's all. Just the same,' he added, 'we'd better not pick the smallest size they've got.'

That night, driving the car, Stan added many a flourish to the signals of the highway code, and Esther, feeling the breeze on her face, reflected that she had never seen him in quite the same mood of optimism.

The immediate past, until tonight a pattern for their future, seemed now to have been merely a preliminary course for beginners. Soon, she thought, Stan would have what he had always needed—solid foundations, people, places of his own, demands, responsibilities. He would enter the normal world of the Maitlands and their fellows. Graduate.

Stan stopped whistling to say, 'What should we get

first, Est? House or kids?…House, I guess.' Pulling up at a red light he said, 'You do want *two*, don't you?'

'If we can have them. All at once, like this, it's hard to imagine any, but I think you're right that two would be best.'

Chortling away, Stan accelerated as the lights changed. In a minute he said, 'Old Clem'll think we're lost…Do you think we should see someone about all this? David, maybe? After all, he's a solicitor or something, isn't he? He should know about these things. Might be able to get it fixed up faster. Pull a few strings.'

'I know he would be very happy to help us. I'm sure he could tell us what we should do,' she said steadily, but Stan guessed her reaction. Magnanimously confirming his offer he said, 'I'll go in to his office tomorrow. Bet it'll surprise him.' He gave a short laugh. 'It'll surprise a few so-and-sos.'

They cruised along the tree-lined street looking for a parking place. The nickel and bright duco of American cars gleamed under the lights.

'I'll ring David in the morning and tell him you're coming,' Esther said, as they walked back towards the hotel. 'But I'd rather not mention it to Clem tonight.'

'You are keen on this, aren't you, Est?'

She touched his hand and they slowed, dawdled lover-like for a few steps until the sound of music coming from the hotel reminded them of their obligations, and with sudden belated compunction they began to hurry.

172

The office was cool, even chill, after the heat outside. Stan sat in a deep leather chair and inspected the room while he waited for David to see him. Five minutes, his secretary had said. Now she was tapping efficiently on her typewriter, occupied and withdrawn, and next to her, on the other side of the polished wooden fence, another girl, a blonde—Clem's secretary, he supposed— sat at her machine.

Neither of the girls had looked up, or spoken, or slackened pace for an instant since he had established his identity and picked up a copy of *Punch*. The smooth, shining heads remained slightly averted to the left, the hands raced.

The clack of typewriter keys had a peaceful effect in the high, white-walled room. Dark wood, gleaming floor and furniture, fresh flowers, electric light and the snap of machines. Stan seldom found himself in such surroundings. He felt he was being sapped and subdued by them until he cleared his throat noisily—so noisily as to make the girls look up—to reassert his personality. Behind the glum façade he was jittery.

In his imagination he rehearsed the scene to come. His voice was gruff and matter-of-fact. That was the way to be, he decided. And then when he had it all taped he'd ring Est. Pity he had to see Connelly about those blueprints; he'd have gone straight home, otherwise. Still, Connelly was just back from the States. He'd have news. After they'd had a talk he could collect Est and go and see whoever David said. Maybe look at some houses.

Voices came from the other office. Someone was coming out. A stout man who had, a moment before, been a dark grey shadow behind the opaque glass-panelled door, came from David's office. He glanced at Stan, and, as he passed the girls, nodded good morning.

Stan wished again that he was seeing David somewhere else. Against his will these austere chambers overpowered him. However, here he was, like it or not.

The girl said something. 'Would you come this way, please, Mr Peterson? Mr Prescott will see you now.' She closed the door behind him.

'Hello, David.'

'Sit down, Stan. I'm sorry I kept you waiting.' The apology was automatic. 'I'm glad you came in today.

I suppose Esther told you that I was on the point of ringing to suggest the same thing when she spoke to me?'

'Yes, she said something about it.'

David sat at a desk, his back to a sheet of windows. One wall of his office was lined with books. There were some engravings in narrow black frames. A thick, dark-blue carpet covered the floor. Stan noticed these details and gathered a general impression of order and space.

Removing his spectacles, David laid them on a stack of papers on the desk in front of him. As he spoke he watched the circles of light reflected through them.

'My business with you can wait for a few minutes. Tell me, what kind of information is it that you want? Esther preferred not to mention it on the phone.'

Stan fixed his eyes on the pattern of light that still held David's attention. 'Well,' he began, and was thankful to hear his voice, gruff and matter-of-fact, continuing with the story just as he had planned. He was relieved. It was much easier than he had expected. David made no sound or movement until he came to a halt.

When it was all told, Stan allowed himself a sheepish grin—indeed, he could not restrain it; for there it was in a nutshell. They planned to get a house and two kids. Yes, it had to be two; and they wanted to get them at the same time. As to age, they weren't so fussy, but the boy had to be a bit older than the girl. And now, the point was, who should they see? How long would it take? And could he use a bit of influence to hurry it up and cut out the red tape?

Stan fell back in his chair and crossed his legs. Then he leaned forward with his cigarette case. When David shook his head, he sat back again, at ease for the first time that morning.

'Well? What do you think?' he asked when the smoke was streaming from his cigarette. 'You look surprised, all right. Knew you would be.'

David raised his head. 'I *am* surprised,' he said with quiet emphasis, 'and if what I have been told is correct, I shall be more than surprised, I shall be disgusted.' He put on his spectacles and clasped his hands in front of him.

Freezing into stillness, Stan said angrily, 'What the hell are you talking about?'

'Just this. I've had a visit from an ex-employee of yours, and, I regret to say, of mine...'

'Jeffries.'

'I have no admiration for the man. He may have lied to me. He obviously bears you a grudge and wants to injure you. As a rule such witnesses are not reliable, or shall I say, not completely reliable. Hatred can produce a view of the truth so obliquely distorted that one is never sure again of the ground in question. There must always be doubts.' He paused for a moment and met Stan's eyes. 'In this case, however, Jeffries was dealing with facts—a great many facts. Was he speaking the truth?'

Trying bravado, Stan answered insolently, 'Depends a bit what he said, doesn't it? Anyhow, you're so good at it, you tell me.'

'I thought so.'

Only the subdued clatter of the outer office broke the silence.

'According to Jeffries, every detail of the business you conduct is illegal. You manufacture without licence. You ignore copyright. You have contempt for laws regulating imports and exports.' He went on, 'You appear to find opportunities for gain during every consumer shortage the city suffers. Indeed, Jeffries credits you with the ability to create these gluts and shortages in order to turn them to your own advantage. New regulations of all kinds appear to inspire your ingenuity, so that you are at the same time able to overcome them, and increase profit.' David stopped again and looked at Stan, who eyed him derisively.

'So Jeffries said all that, did he? Blah! Blah! Quite a mouthful!' He imitated David's portentous manner. 'He must have come on a bit if he said all that.' He snickered at his own humour. 'And just what are you going to do about it, anyhow, Mr Prescott? Not that I'm saying I'm as smart as all that, mind you.'

'I'm going to ask you to give up this method of making money,' David said steadily.

'Ha! That's a laugh! Ask away, Mr Prescott!' He suddenly dropped the pose of cocky assurance and leaned forward, his face contorted. 'He told you nothing. He couldn't prove a thing. The dirty little—'

'All right, all right. That will do,' David checked him abruptly. 'You don't seem to understand. You are not being threatened. I realise very well that you are not likely to have allowed conclusive evidence—in the way of papers and so forth—to leave your person.'

'Huh! Papers!' Stan scoffed and tapped his head. 'It's all in here!'

'In any case, from what he says, it seems clear that the police are aware of your activities—certain of them, at any rate. I doubt if much that Jeffries or I might say would be new to them, and if it were, I should not inform against you.'

'I bet. Look good, wouldn't it? "Notable Solicitor Sends Brother-in-Law to Quod."' He laughed. 'Don't worry, Mr Prescott. You won't have the chance. They haven't been able to get anything on me yet, and they won't!'

David waited, and then, looking down, he asked, 'What does Esther know?'

'It's no concern of hers,' Stan drawled. 'The trouble with Jeffries was he didn't know when he was well off. Starting to give me advice. Starting to get too interested.'

'I'm talking about Esther.'

'Are you? What about her?' Stan sneered, but his confidence was beginning to ebb.

David rubbed his forehead wearily. 'I blame myself that she ever married you. I should have made more inquiries. I should have done a lot of things. What I'm asking you now is to give this up for her sake, if not your own, before you *are* involved with the police. You still have a chance. You aren't old. You must have money, and, I suppose, some kind of ability—though God knows it's been put to poor enough use.'

Stan gnawed at his thumbnail, remembering the good intentions he had had when he married Esther. He just hadn't got around to doing anything about them yet, that was all. 'Why should I give it up? What harm does it do?' he asked sulkily, like a reprimanded schoolboy.

'Ask yourself that. You'll know best.' David began to hope. 'There can be no peace in the kind of life you lead. It's unnatural—it's all wrong,' he urged.

The telephone at his elbow tinkled, and they became aware that they were in a square, light room, high above the traffic. They found that they were more than voices and emotions existing in featureless space.

Stan shifted his position restlessly, and his mouth hardened in a downward curving line as David lifted the receiver.

'Yes?...I thought I told you not to put calls through, Miss Burnett?...Very well.'

As they faced each other again, David saw by Stan's expression that he had lost his case, and with this knowledge came a slackening of effort. His shoulders sagged a little. 'What have you decided?'

'That you should mind your own bloody business and let me mind mine!'

David gave him a level look and clenched his teeth. 'And you came here to tell me that you want to adopt two children! I suppose I shouldn't be surprised. At least that fact convinces me that Esther hasn't taken the trouble to find out exactly how you support her. I hardly think she would have agreed to this plan if she had.'

'Well, you're wrong if you think this'll make any difference to her. Try to mess things up for me and see how you get on. You won't see her again.'

'I could wish you deserved her affection more.'

'Well!' Stan jeered, surprised by the tacit admission of his power. 'There's nothing you can do, is there? Or do you plan to tell her anyhow, just for the hell of it?'

David was unbearably provoked by the tone in Stan's voice that suggested that in some curious way he was gratified by the morning's events. And he did, in fact, feel a vicious satisfaction in no longer hiding the truth from David. The Prescotts, the mighty Prescotts, were dismayed, and a siren song of malice echoed in his brain.

'Well,' he prodded. 'Are you going to tell her?'

'I don't know,' David said. 'But I'll tell you one thing: don't try to adopt any children through any channels whatever, for I'll see to it that you don't succeed.

I thank God that you haven't any of your own. What a father they'd have had,' he said bitterly. 'A racketeer, a gambler, a cheat!'

'Hey! Hey!' Stan stuttered, starting up from his chair, incensed. 'Watch what you're saying! I won't take much more of this, you know.' He was undone with rage and mortification to find that, after all, he still had points to lose. In the midst of his fury he could have whimpered. Racketeer, gambler, cheat, what a father...

Blindly, through waves of hurt and shame, he floundered around for invective that would paralyse the man in front of him, but for once he failed to find it.

'Remember what I've said. Be satisfied that you've involved my sister in your unsavoury life and don't try to drag children into the mess. The only other thing I have to say to you is: see that you treat Esther well. I'll leave it to you to think of an explanation for the failure of your scheme. I'll make sure that I don't speak to her until you've had time to tell her. And you'd better let me know what you've said.'

Already David was regretting his outburst. The thought that he was, however unwillingly, instrumental in denying Esther the right to children was painful. Now it was too late to retract, and Esther had wanted the children—not only Stan. How would he tell her?

He had been looking down at his desk, but now he raised his head and gazed at Stan, who stood transfixed with hatred.

At last, speaking thickly, with cold intensity, Stan said, 'I'd like to see you dead!' He stood where he was a moment longer, then, wheeling round, strode out of the room and shut the door with a crash.

Clem came in as the outer door of the office banged, and his eyes questioned David as he seated himself on the edge of the desk.

'I went too far,' David said. 'I completely lost my temper. I should have let you handle it—you've always got on better with him. If I'd known why he was coming—they wanted to adopt some children...'

His brother screwed up his face. 'Oh Lord!'

'It was a good sign, wasn't it? You'd have thought I'd have bargained with him—the situation was perfect for it. But I didn't. Miss Burnett phoned through when I thought I had him...After that it was impossible: we were both abusive, and I was moral...'

Stan couldn't remember leaving the office, but suddenly he was outside. The humid air closed about him like a blanket wrung out in hot water. It was mildly comforting. He looked around with an angry, startled gaze, too distracted for a second to understand where he was. Then he knew. Near Martin Place. He crossed the road, relying on his fury to keep off the oncoming traffic, yet so lifted out of himself that he would have welcomed the chance to savage cars and occupants.

Forging through the lunchtime crowds, he reached the car and stood with his foot on the running board, but after a tumult of indecision he jerked back on to the footpath and pushed his way along to the Golden Reef. There, amidst the buzzing and the raucous shouts, with the sweet, beery smell, a glass in his hand and some whisky in his mouth, he could think and plan. But not straightaway, he counselled. Have a few first. Clear your head. He felt his chest contract with hate and high, wounded pain. I'll get even with that little...I'll...

A large ginger cat appeared and began to twine itself around his legs, knowing instinctively where it was not wanted. Smooth, smooth. It purred.

Looking down Stan saw it and lifted his foot with a jerk that sent the cat across the floor. It stalked to the other end of the bar, and, faintly mollified, Stan picked up his glass.

As he finished his drink and turned to order another, there was a knock on his back. A small man with fair hair and round blue eyes tapped patiently on his spine as if it were a door. Stan inspected him contemptuously.

'Shouldn't 'a done that, mate,' the little man said. 'I saw you deliberately kick that kitty and shouldn't 'a done it. Never done you any harm, did it? Nice kitty.' He smiled ingratiatingly into Stan's eyes. 'You won't do it again, though, will you, mate?...Mate? Will you?' Stan turned his back on him. 'Aw...' The little man's eyes filled with tears. 'He won't do it again. He didn't mean it.' But no one was listening. No one cared at all.

Towards evening Stan moved on to the Bricklayers Arms, where he stayed until closing time. By then he had forgotten where he had left the car—forgotten that he owned a car. He caught a taxi home.

CHAPTER EIGHTEEN

Rachel had said goodbye to her aunt and uncle before going to work in the morning.

'It's not as if you were in a house by yourself,' Pauline Demster had said, unconvinced. 'There are people all around you. You won't be nervous, will you, dear?'

'Heavens, no!' Rachel lied, raising her eyebrows in disgust.

'And Mrs Maitland and Esther would help you if anything went wrong. And you'll be seeing Luigi,' Pauline said. 'The pantry has enough food in it for six months, I think, so you'll be all right for everything except fruit and vegs and so on. And everything's labelled, so you can't make any mistakes with your cooking...'

'Yes, I know. Everything will be fine.'

When she came home at night, they had gone, and the flat was quiet and unwelcoming and horribly tidy. Stocks—or were they phlox?—sitting about in vases, looking as if she had interrupted their conversation, and the clock ticking. In the kitchen the refrigerator was throbbing in a subdued, peaceful way; the taps over the sink were hot with captured sunlight.

Rachel tried to make the rooms seem peopled by visiting them all frequently. She tested Pauline's and Robert's chairs and studied the sitting room from these unfamiliar angles. At length, having by a breathless feat of balancing achieved the simultaneous readiness of tray, omelette, toast, coffee and fruit salad, she kicked off her sandals and, putting her feet up on the sofa, prepared to eat her dinner in the fashion of the Ancient Greeks.

All that's missing is the garland of ivy and violets, she thought regretfully. And the wine, and the company. And the slaves, she added, as she trotted back to the kitchen for the salt that she had forgotten.

While she washed the dishes, she played Crosby and Sinatra records on her old gramophone, rushing every three minutes to choose a new song. The tunes compelled her to join in, made her hands move more and more slowly until she ceased altogether to rub the dry cloth on the wet plates. An enveloping, hugging movement was all that could be attempted without loss of art, and with that, the dishes, perforce, were finished. The gramophone was closed up; she got out her books, pen and ink, and began.

She had been working for hours, absorbed, but now, for the last fifteen minutes the thought of Luigi had been hanging between her and the beginning of the Peloponnesian War. She looked at her watch and saw that it was late. It was too bad to read with a divided mind.

Yawning, she closed the history book, the classical atlas and the volume of Thucydides. She stretched lazily, relaxed, and smiled affectionately at them.

'You were a good man,' she said aloud to Thucydides, as she went over to the bookcase. 'And wise. The same thing according to Socrates.' She stood for a moment reflecting on her good fortune in finding compatibility with Socrates. But she was tired and it was late and there was work tomorrow. She must go to bed. She wondered very cautiously if everything was locked, knowing that it was, but wondering nevertheless.

The reading lamp over her bed clicked out and she pulled the sheet up to her chin. She would not listen for noises. She would think about the picnic they were going to have on Saturday. They would go in the old car, and take the gramophone, and she would only speak in Italian, yes, really...

She thanked heaven for the streetlight that shone into her room, and thought about her aunt and uncle

187

in Hobart, their bedroom here so uncannily stripped and bare.

Someone moved in the flat overhead and she lay tense, suddenly cold. Then, identifying the sound, she grew limp, and felt foolish and annoyed. Turning and twisting ostentatiously in the bed to show her indifference to the robbers and murderers who might be all around her, at last she fell asleep.

Bright-eyed, olive-skinned people filled her dreams. She was with them on an island that floated on an indigo sea. White marble columns shone against the sky, and there was the sound of flutes in the distance. Salty and fresh, a breeze blew in from the sea, bringing, so it seemed, a feeling of great joy...

CHAPTER NINETEEN

She was out of bed on her feet before she knew what had happened. Eyes enormous, senses quivering, she listened. Yes, there it was again, that frantic tapping on the door that had wakened her. One o'clock, the luminous hands of the clock said. She swallowed nervously and stood, lips parted, muscles rigid.

The paperweight would be something. She jerked herself to life, picked it up, put it down as she struggled into her dressing gown, trying to hurry. Then it was in her hand again, heavy and solid.

The lights came on silently, negotiated as much by nerves and will as by the careful plastic fingers that touched the switches with intuitive pressure.

Heart beating with thick uneven bumps, she crept to the hall. Still the frenzied rapping on the door. A murderer would be quieter—unless he guessed that she would think so and was trying to trap her. Her eyes tested the strength of the Yale lock, and the small brass bolt.

Suddenly she called, 'Who's there?' Her voice was harsh, unnatural.

'It's Esther. Please let me in, Rachel.'

'Esther?' she repeated incredulously. She gave a great sigh and rushed to get rid of the paperweight and unlock the door.

Inside, while Rachel closed and bolted it again, Esther smiled at her back, addressed it while one hand went out to the wall for support.

She said, 'I'm so sorry to wake you up this time of night. I must have given you an awful fright. You're by yourself, aren't you?'

'Yes.' Rachel turned to answer her, limp with relief, waiting for an explanation, but when she looked at Esther's face she asked no questions.

Esther endured the eyes on her face for a few seconds, and then said, 'Yes...Would you mind if I stayed here tonight?' Would it be a great nuisance?' They had moved slowly into the other room, were sitting down now, and she added, 'If I could perhaps stay here on the sofa?'

'Yes, of course, stay. I'll make one of the beds for you.'

'I'd rather stay here.'

190

Rachel folded her dressing gown over her knees, looked up at Esther, distressed. 'Oh, what can I get you?' she said helplessly.

'Nothing, nothing. There's nothing wrong.' She half raised a hand to her bruised face, and gave a laugh that made tears spring to Rachel's eyes. 'I'm sure it looks much worse than it is—really.'

'Oh,' Rachel gave an involuntary wail of fright and shock. 'I'll make some tea,' she said and ran through to the kitchen, wiping her eyes on the sash of her gown, rubbing her left forearm across her eyes as she held the kettle under the tap.

Alone, Esther lay back on the sofa, drew a quivering breath, and the handbag she had been tightly holding slipped to the floor. 'Oh dear...oh dear...' The mild exclamations came from her almost voicelessly. She bent her head to her cupped hands and breathed again.

The tea was never drunk, but its entry, Rachel coming in with the tray, made Esther rouse herself to say: 'You ought to go back to bed now. You have to go to work in the morning. I really shouldn't have come like this, but I had to go somewhere. And don't,' she shook her head slightly and frowned, 'don't think about this. You see, it was—I don't quite know what happened—but—'

Quite suddenly her composure broke and she said incredulously, 'Stan hit me, punched me. Oh, he hurt me...Yes, yes, he did!' she protested. She stopped

191

abruptly and looked at Rachel, awed. She stared at her for a long time, then the memory came sharply again, and she gave a little laughing moan, a hysterical mingling of pain and disbelief.

Distracted with pity, Rachel hovered around, 'Oh, don't! Oh, don't!' she said. 'Will you have some tea?... Oh, what can I do?'

'He shouldn't have spoken to me like that, should he? He really shouldn't.' Then, as if the speechless Rachel had agreed with her, she said, 'But you're not to think— he would never go to another woman, I know that—it was my brother David and the adoption...Something happened, I don't know what. He was drunk when he did this. He didn't know. He doesn't know what he's done.' After a silence she went on, painfully, more slowly now, 'You see, I'm telling you this—because—I don't want you to think that this means—anything— that we don't love each other...'

Rachel looked blank and Esther gave a faint smile. 'Oh, I know, I know. But you're young,' she said. And then, dropping the role of the older, wiser woman, she said confidingly, smiling, with the memory sending tears to her eyes, 'He's always said, "I wouldn't let a cold wind blow on you, pet, if I could help it..." Don't you think?'

A sudden awareness caused her to touch her mouth almost furtively. She sat looking heavily at the thin smear of blood on her fingers, then closed her eyes.

In the middle of the floor in front of the weeping woman, Rachel looked hopelessly round the room for something that might help. This should never have happened to Esther, she thought, not to someone like her.

'He didn't mean to…He didn't know what he was doing.' She repeated Esther's words.

'No. He wanted to.'

It was half-past two, and Rachel's head ached. She was stiff from standing so long in the same position, but it seemed to her that if, by so much as a movement to sit down, she made Esther more aware of herself, reminded her of all that she had said, then she, Rachel, would have failed completely to act as an adult should in such a situation.

Later, before she went to bed, Rachel promised to set the alarm clock for six. Esther said, 'I mustn't sleep. I must go upstairs early in the morning before people start moving about.'

'Of course,' Rachel nodded, then added hesitantly, 'Do you think you should? I mean, will it be all right? You could stay here. I'll be out all day.'

But Esther seemed agitated at the idea. 'No, no, thank you. I must go home.'

Drugged with weariness, but unable to sleep, Rachel lay watching the sky lighten, peering through the half-light occasionally with stinging eyes to see if Esther had perhaps gone, or if she slept.

When the sky was bright she staggered dazedly through to the other room, and Esther was up at once, collecting her handbag, refusing breakfast, her desire to be gone as strong as her need, the night before, for sanctuary.

At the door, remembering, she looked at Rachel drearily. She felt that she could harbour neither hopes nor cares as to the attitude of her listener. But looking at Rachel's tired, strained face, a small sensation of relief swept over her.

'Would you mind not...?'

'I won't ever...'

That afternoon Esther spoke to David on the telephone in a bright social voice.

'Stan suggested that I should ask you, David. He seems to feel that the difficulty is a technicality that you might be able to overcome?'

She wanted to scream at him: 'What happened when he saw you? What did you do to him?' She wanted to hurt herself physically until someone answered her questions, maim herself, but instead, she held the receiver, stared at the wall, waited.

After a hesitation David's voice came, faintly shocked. 'It was rather more than that, my dear. I'm truly sorry that I can't help you, Esther, but it would be quite impossible.' When she did not reply he said, 'Stan said nothing more to you?'

'No!' she said, with a touch of nervous asperity. 'And really, David, I'm rather tired of being sent to first one and then the other to discover something that surely concerns me as much as anyone. I really won't have it,' she said weakly, with a hint of tears. She was immediately stiff with fear in case her brother had noticed.

'You're right, of course...I'd come round to have a talk with you about it, but I feel that I should leave it to Stan.' He paused again. 'However...I think I'd better come on Tuesday afternoon, Esther.' He added in a lower, muffled tone, 'Until then, believe that I am sorry about the adoption, my dear, please.'

What does it matter about the adoption? she thought feverishly. It mattered once, but you've damaged something of much greater importance.

'Very well, David,' she said flatly. 'I'll expect you on Tuesday.'

But before Tuesday Stan had changed his mind, and given her his version of the scene in David's office. He was only half-drunk when he told her—but drunk enough to be fluent and biting. Esther reacted instinctively with absolute silence, knowing that he watched eagerly for any movement that suggested she was about to argue or contradict him.

'Go on! Go on!' he urged, his eyes glittering with anticipation.

But she sat motionless and quiet, protecting them both from the violent scene he craved. Unable to force her into a collision that would have sheltered him, he nevertheless told her what had happened. Listening to his voice, watching his eyes, she was bereft of feeling. She was conscious only of slow, thumping heartbeats, of breathing. Looking down, she saw the body, the arms and legs of the creature she was, and knew that solidity was an illusion.

So that's it, she thought, unmoved by Stan's admission of his activities, thinking only of the way in which David had handled his knowledge. Stan quietened down after he had told her, later he went out.

All day Esther thought about it, dispassionately. So that's it. The following morning she rang her brother.

'You needn't bother to come round tomorrow,' she said. 'I know what happened.'

'Oh?' David said, relieved but apprehensive. 'I'll come just the same, Esther, to talk things over with you.'

'No—don't.'

He tried to laugh to show that he did not take her seriously.

'I don't want to see you, David.'

'Surely you must agree that I have some interest in the matter? It was my duty to speak to him. Don't let this make any difference to us. This isn't like you, my dear.'

She smiled at that.

'Are you there?'

196

'You had no right to speak to him. You should have told me if you felt you had to do anything at all...What do you know of the kind of life he's had to make for himself? You've always disliked him.'

'Esther, please...' David said helplessly. After a pause, he asked, 'If I am not to come to see you, may I ring again in a day or so?'

'If you must. What are you going to do in the meantime,' she asked in a voice that startled them both, 'hold a family conference to discuss Stan's shortcomings? Arrange a divorce? Try to have him deported?' She scored the cream-painted telephone table with a long thumbnail in her distaste for herself and David and Stan and her remarks. 'All right, David,' she sighed. 'I'm sorry. Ring when you want to. There's nothing else to say just now, is there?'

'Goodbye, Esther. I hope this hasn't made any trouble between you. That wasn't my intention. But I was right to tackle him. I think he may take some notice even yet—and then you'll realise what a good thing it was that I did...'

At first Esther moved the listening end of the receiver from her ear, then she hung up. She went from room to room and opened the windows wide, for the air was stale and reeked of spirits. The Monday morning mess seemed worse than usual—dead flowers, empty bottles, spotty carpet. Stan didn't eat very tidily when he was drinking; there was grease, probably butter, on the arm of his chair. Yes, but he had been sober this morning, and quiet, and she had snapped and worried at him. Oh, it wasn't surprising; but she, as the one with some knowledge and control, was the one to exercise these qualities. She was the one who should try.

She wandered onto the balcony and looked over to the tall buildings and busy, blue harbour. The sun soothed her and made her shiver. She sat down tiredly and gazed into the sky. After a time the fingers of one hand pressed against her forehead and she leaned forward to ease the pain in her chest.

CHAPTER TWENTY

Vi looked up at the reflection in the mirror and put down her powder-puff.

'Well!' she said, breathless with shock. 'You've got a nerve! What do you think you're doing here?'

'Your day off, isn't it?'

'What's it to you if it is? Do you know just how many weeks it is since you took any interest in my time off?' she asked bitterly. 'I do.'

Stan gazed back in a considering fashion, but kept silent.

'Well! Where've you been? Make a few excuses,' she said, powdering her face again to hide her agitation.

'Binge,' he said laconically.

Vi gave a short laugh. 'For weeks? I never noticed you keeping clear of me before because you'd had too much.' But she turned round and looked at him closely. 'How did you get in here, anyhow?'

'Key. You gave me one, remember?'

Vi looked at him for a moment and took a deep breath. 'Do *I* remember?' She stretched out first one leg and then the other to straighten the seams of her stockings. 'That's good! Do *I* remember?' She smoothed her thick blonde hair with rough, jerking hands. 'Oh, God,' she cried, 'I remember too damned many things— that's my trouble. I wish I'd never seen you again after that last time, Stan. If you'd thought of anyone but yourself you'd never have gone away, or you'd never have come back. But you don't care about me. You don't care how often you come or go as long as I'm here when you want me. It doesn't matter what happens to me in between. I'm unlucky. I'm different. I can't forget people as easily as you.'

Her clenched fist went to her heart instinctively, to beat against it, to convince him that she meant what she said, that she spoke what she felt, that she was talking about herself, Vi Rogers, and that he had to listen.

'We've been together a lot over the years. I know you. I'm used to you. I've never expected much from you or kidded myself...but I'm human, too, you're not the only one in the world, and when you started with me again like that, you shouldn't have gone away. Though why I *care*...'

Holding his head in his hands, Stan listened to her gloomily, muttering to himself. When she stopped he said weakly, 'Be yourself, Vi! You're never short of—' he caught her eye and finished, 'friends.'

Vi sat at the dressing table, her back to the mirror, watching him. At his words she stood up. 'That's just as well, isn't it? Go away, Stan. Go away, and don't come back. I've had enough of you.'

There's something about her, Stan thought, surprised as always, after a separation from Vi, to find that he had missed her, that his feelings were, after all, more deeply involved than he had remembered. And he had been so convinced that coming here today was an act designed to even things up with David Prescott. That now appeared to be only partly true.

He sat down on the bed and watched her blow her nose and wipe her eyes. She combed her hair and fixed her make-up. When she had finished she turned and looked at him for a moment or two, trying to guess his intentions.

'Look, will you just *go*!…All right, if you won't, I will,' she said, and went to the wardrobe for her hat.

Stan saw that she meant it and he jumped to his feet to block the doorway. 'Don't be a silly goat,' he said roughly. 'You haven't given a man a chance to say anything.'

'Huh!' she laughed ironically. 'I suppose I've given a man a chance to think of something by now…Okay.

I'm listening.' She let her straw hat fall to the floor and sat down.

He spoke and moved towards her at the same time. 'I've had a hell of a lot of trouble over a big deal all this time, Vi. I've been in a pretty bad spot or I'd have been round same as usual. You know that.'

'Oh, sure. I know I can count on you.' But while she doubted, and raised scornful eyebrows, she experienced a jolt of alarm. Any trouble could be really bad for Stan—and his luck had been too consistent.

He sat down beside her. 'Everything's settled now,' he said, 'but it was sticky while it lasted. Afterwards I just felt like a binge.'

Concern overcoming scepticism, Vi said, 'You ought to be careful. A fellow called Jeffries has been going on about you down at the pub. I've had to get Joe to shut him up a few times.'

Her blue eyes searched the expressionless black pupils and brown iris as long as Stan would allow— for seconds only—before he flickered the short brown lashes restlessly and turned his head.

Was he lying? Wasn't he? She could detect no sign of change in the smooth-shaven texture of his skin, in the doubtful lines of his mouth. And yet some inner nerve told her that he had seen a crisis, that in the other life of his, an event had happened—something she would not discover.

Stan put his hand under her chin and kissed her on

the mouth, slowly, deliberately. Her airless lungs, her weary, listless heart sent arms and weight to resist him. She tried to push him away, feeling cold and lifeless, unwilling to be roused. But Stan held her firmly until he felt her weaken, relax, and respond at last with the unhappy passion of desperation.

Later, she said slowly, 'You didn't get very far with your excuses.'

'Are you complaining?' Stan asked, putting down her hairbrush and looking at himself in the mirror.

She held out a hand. 'Come to the kitchen. We'll make some coffee.'

Stan grinned. Arms round each other they angled through the doorway and joggled with uneven steps down the short passage to the red-and-white kitchen.

Soon the coffee was percolated and poured, and Stan, dunking a doughnut, watched with interest as part of the fat, golden circle turned dark and the sugar coating melted. He dived at it and caught the soggy bit before it fell.

He waved the remaining portion at Vi approvingly. 'Damned good—I'm hungry.'

She took a bit of hers and said, 'Don't they feed you, honey?' undoing in a second months of caution— months during which she never asked 'why' or 'when', during which she was his accomplice in an act of deception meant to deceive only herself.

'That's enough of that!' Stan rapped at her, casting

down the uneaten doughnut, chewing his last mouthful as if it had suddenly turned to sand.

'All right, all right,' Vi said, trying to look indifferent to his rebuke until the shock left her. She drank her coffee, and they sat in heavy silence until she had finished.

'Let's forget it?'

Stan gave her a cigarette. 'Well! What now?'

She glanced at the clock. 'Hell! We'd better clear out of here in a minute or there'll be someone at the door looking for me. I was going out with a friend. And I said a friend, Stan.'

'I heard you. Why'd you have to say it twice?'

'Funny!'

'Too bad about your friend. Where'll we go? Got any ideas?'

'Have you got the car? Can we drive out of town somewhere?'

'It's what we always do, isn't it? We'll go up Gosford way.'

'Where they grow the oranges? Will they be on the trees now?'

'God knows. We'll see soon enough when we get there.'

'It's a great day, Stany,' Vi said, encouragingly.

'Is it?' He squinted out of the window, looking consciously at the sky for the first time for weeks. 'Yeah, not bad,' he complimented her as if she had made it. He opened the door. 'Well, come on, tiger.' He rattled the car keys and they were out of the flat and down the stairs, joking, suddenly laughing. By the time Vi's doorbell rang, they were on the Pacific Highway heading north out of town towards the Hawkesbury River and the orchards of Gosford.

They had a good day. Once outside the city limits, Stan urged the car forward, the speedometer needle flickering between sixty and eighty. Vi threw her hat on the back seat, screwed down the window and turned to him, laughing, exhilarated by sun and wind and speed, the sick depression of the last weeks gone entirely now that he was back again. They talked mostly about old times, which pleased Stan. It gave him a sense of continuity to be able to reminisce with Vi. The boys, the original boys, had drifted away, coming and going, not to be relied on: Vi was the only consistent link with the old days. She was there when the gang won a pile on Tickety and went on the razzle. When they were all working up north, she was in the boat that time it capsized, and helped to hold old Salty Marshall up till the other boat came. She was there when he started out in business on his own, and she'd been full of ideas to help him.

When they reached the great, island-strewn river, they left the car for a while before crossing. On the hilly, tree-laden bank a few spaces had been cleared, and here there were stalls selling potato chips and ice-cream and soft drinks and oysters.

Stan bought oysters and they ate them from the bottle with their fingers as they wandered around, leaned on the white railings, looked up and down the river, whose water was grey-blue and choppy, like the sea. A train passed over the long railway bridge on its way north.

Vi wiped her fingers when the oysters were finished and gazed around in a state of deep, thoughtless content. Stan breathed the air in in lung-cooling gulps, and, when he thought she would not notice, he looked at Vi, more aware of her, more appreciative of her vital strength and warm glamour than he had been for years.

They crossed the river and, reaching Gosford soon afterwards, left the main road and drove down dusty yellow country roads, past farms and orchards and guesthouses, past miles of gum trees, over little wooden bridges spanning dried-up creeks. Presently they came to a valley where small, brilliant birds darted from tree to tree, flashing, dipping, making Vi exclaim and call to Stan to stop the car.

He dragged a rug from the boot and walking a short distance into the bush, found a grassy clearing, where he spread the tartan square and flopped down. The earth was baked dry and warm; the trees moved overhead in the breeze. It was very quiet. There was an occasional birdcall. Around them, all was transparent sunshine and green shade.

They drank some beer and Stan slept for half an hour or so with one arm thrown over his eyes. When he woke and moved, he saw Vi looking down at him, her eyes as blue as the birds, and he put a hand up to give her cheek a rough pat.

'A kookaburra laughed and woke you,' she said. 'Now stay awake and talk to me.'

Yawning and stretching, warm and lazy, after a time they wandered back through the maze of grey-green scrub and silver gums, liking the scented air, catching some sense of the lonely spaces, the brooding apprehension of the bush.

It was late when Stan let himself into the flat that night, but Esther was at the end of the hall waiting for him.

'Hello, Est.' He gave her a kiss on the cheek.

'You must be tired. Can I get you something to eat?'

'No, thanks.' He lowered himself wearily into a chair and lit a cigarette. 'Had a big day. Had to be in about six places at once. Finished up carting stuff round about eight o'clock.'

She believed him. Occasionally she went with him in the car, and she knew the routine of visits to suburban bungalows, knew that it took time, and that at the factory Eddie and Eck were always worried and harassed, up to their eyes in work.

She sat on the edge of her chair with her arms extended and her hands on her knees like a young girl trying to appear relaxed. 'I'm sorry if I was cross this morning, Stan. I didn't mean to be...'

'Were you cross?' Stan said, pulling some papers from his pocket. 'Didn't notice, pet...You look dead beat, you know. You look as if you could do with an early night.'

'It's a little late for an early night, but I am tired.'

'Why don't you just go along, then? I'll be a while yet. Got some things to do.'

The bruises had faded from her face and the cut on her lip had healed. Since the day Stan had told her about his meeting with David there had been no reference to that scene, nor to the one which had succeeded it, in their own flat. On the same occasion, by way of a conclusion, Stan had thrown in a casual apology, a few words, grudgingly, slanting with recrimination. Three days after that he left a thin wad of notes on her dressing table. A present.

Tonight he was quite sober, quite amiable, yet how far apart they seemed. Flat-faced strangers.

Plumping up the cushions as she rose, she frowned fretfully, remembering her irritable outburst this morning, and the day before, and quite a few days back. She called up the high, sharp note of her voice, the feeble petulance of her words, as a punishment and warning. She would not do it again. She really wouldn't. And if they both tried...

After Esther had gone to bed Stan jumped up and began to pace about the room, his hands in his pockets and a smirk on his face. He gazed at the walls and the carpet and the furniture in an ecstasy of self-satisfaction, as if they were animated and paying him homage.

They were good kids, he thought indulgently. There was no doubt, either, he was pretty important to them both. Quite a boy. He grinned slightly to himself. Calling Esther a kid. He chuckled and had to cover his mouth with his hand. It wouldn't do if she heard him laughing.

He grew serious again. Poor old Est. She wasn't looking too good these days, and getting herself worked up about nothing all the time. It wasn't any wonder, though. He'd given her a pretty rough trot one way and another. He'd have to make it up to her somehow. It wasn't her fault that that so-and-so of a brother of hers had such a big mouth.

Remorse weighed on him: he pouted and frowned. But the pang of disgust he experienced was not unmixed with more agreeable sensations.

However, some work! He had plenty to do after taking a day off like that, right in the middle of the week. Still, a man's only human—that's what Vi said.

That day, Bill Maitland had taken Anabel to his sister's house on his way to the office.

Laura had explained about it to her on the telephone. 'Cassie Roberts has this new flat, and she wants me to have a look at it and give her some help about covers and curtains. Don't ask me why, dear.

She's getting it all fixed up instead of going away for a holiday.'

'Is she on holiday now?'

'Yes. We'll have lunch in town after I've seen the place, and I'll get some of my own shopping done then. I can't be bothered going, but I couldn't put her off any longer. I hardly ever have her over now.' Laura shrugged her shoulders. Cassie was the only unmarried woman over thirty that she knew. 'Apart from the fact that we were at school together twenty years ago, God knows what I've got in common with my virginal pal. Still, it's a good deed.'

She had no trouble finding the apartment, and there, when she reached it, was Cass at the door, all anxious and eager because she was fifteen minutes late. Cass looked, to Laura, like an overgrown schoolgirl, with her round face and round brown eyes and her light brown hair and large body. And yet, she was no less good-looking than Laura herself, for Laura had no beauty apart from eyes and hair, but where she glowed, Cass was mild and sexless.

There's no man shortage, either, Laura thought. She, personally, knew several women who could lay claim to more than one man. There was no one but Cass who could claim none. She was pathetic, there was no denying it, and innocent, and good-natured, and in a way, freakish.

'Darling,' she said warmly, kissing her friend, 'it's

lovely to see you again. It's been ages, Cass.' And in a tone of frank appraisal, 'I *love* that dress!'

Cassie flushed with pleasure and led Laura in. They went through the rooms, chatting, admiring proportions, convenience, and one another's clothes in detail; between debates on the merits of gas, as opposed to electric, hot-water systems, discussing their mutual friends.

When they had finished the tour and were sitting on the low divan by the windows, Cassie said solemnly, 'I've got some news for you, Laura. I haven't told anyone else yet.'

'Oh? Out with it!' Laura smiled, adjusted her hat, and waited with royal graciousness. She was confident that it was not a man.

'I'm being sent abroad by the firm for six months, to England and the Continent. I sail next month.'

Laura's eyes went blank as the lens of a camera. 'Why, Cass, that's wonderful!' she exclaimed. 'My dear, I am glad for you. It may be just the thing you're needing. Well, if you aren't the luckiest...*I've* never had the urge to travel.' She laughed to show that she recognised her peculiarity. 'It's just as well, for I don't know when I'd ever get the chance. But anyhow I always feel that there's not much wrong with Australia. A lot of them are glad to come out here—never been so well off in their lives. Still, it will be marvellous for you.'

'Yes, won't it?' Her friend seemed to have lost

interest, and they sat for some time looking at swatches of floral chintzes. Laura chose an attractive pale green cloth with a darker green pattern, which was the one, Cassie admitted when gaily challenged, that she preferred, too.

'Great minds!' sang Laura. 'Shows we've both got good taste.'

It was time to go to town, and they were on the point of leaving when Cassie remembered a letter she had to post. Laura waited in the dim hallway while she went back. She could feel a current of air coming through the half-open front door.

London, Paris, Venice. Her musings were broken up by the sound of voices, and she looked across the oblique angle of the landing, idly curious.

'My God!' she exclaimed under her breath, moving back a little. She stared.

'Stan Peterson and his girl friend!' She was sure of it! Her mouth curved in a deep smile. She felt incredibly enlivened.

Wait till I tell Bill, she thought. And hard on that: I wonder if Esther knows about this? I'll bet one hell of a lot she doesn't.

They had gone by the time Cassie came back with her letter, but the smile lingered on Laura's face. Cassie returned it.

'By the way, I think I saw your neighbour going out. A blonde piece. What's she do?'

212

'Well,' Cassie said, keeping an eye on the traffic as they crossed the road, 'she works at the Cross Keys— I don't know if you know it—a hotel round the corner there.'

'A barmaid?' Oh, it was too much of a cliché, and yet it somehow seemed so *right* for Stan. 'They must be well paid these days if they can afford flats like yours.'

'No,' Cassie said vaguely, 'she's not a barmaid, she—'

'I'll bet she's not.'

They ran for a tram, jumped in and found seats before Cassie said, 'No, what I was going to say about Mrs Rogers was that she's a part-owner. She helps to manage it. She has always been around hotels. Her father used to own one up north.'

'O-oh!'

'It's just that her hair's touched-up,' Cassie said. 'She's been very nice to me since I moved in.'

'I seem to have misjudged the poor woman. She's got a husband, has she?'

Laura paid their fares and the conductor moved off down the corridor.

'No, I don't think so. She's a widow, or else they parted a long time ago...'

'I see.' Laura sighed with respect for Mrs Rogers' possible widowhood. After a moment she said, 'Still, I suppose she won't ever be short of company. That kind of woman never is, eh, Cass?'

213

'I suppose not. I don't know. I like her.'

'It's nice to have nice neighbours,' Laura said, subdued, hoping that her companion had not taken her last remark as containing undertones.

'Here we are—Elizabeth Street.' They left the tram and disappeared into a crowded department store.

CHAPTER TWENTY-ONE

Stan sat in the car outside Romney Court waiting for Esther. He felt slightly sick. His skin was an unhealthy yellowish colour, and his mouth twisted as he ran his tongue over his teeth. He was gazing through the windscreen blindly as he had done for the past ten minutes, conscious of nothing but thickness in head and uncertainty in stomach, when suddenly his eyes focused.

Rachel came out into the street, walked a few steps, turned at the hooting of the horn and saw with some surprise that Stan was signalling her over to the car.

'Like a lift into town? We're going in a minute. Esther's got an early appointment with the hairdresser. Come on, get in,' he said affably.

Desperately unwilling to be alone with them, but not knowing how to refuse his offer, Rachel climbed into the back of the car and sat very stiffly with her white-gloved hands folded neatly over her handbag.

'Bob and Pauline not back yet?' Stan asked, increasing her alarm. He seldom spoke to Rachel; she had always felt herself to be invisible in his company.

'Tomorrow,' she croaked. She cleared her throat and said again, 'They'll be in tomorrow afternoon.'

'Good, good,' Stan said, watching Esther cross the road. 'I—er—asked young Rachel here if she'd like a lift,' he called as if he were warning her.

'That was nice.' She settled herself into the seat and the car moved off. 'How are you, Rachel?' she said coolly, glancing round into the girl's face, not looking at her. 'I haven't seen you for weeks.'

'No,' Rachel murmured, abashed by her tone, conscious that they had not met since the night of the quarrel. 'I'm not at home very much,' she said, hoping that Esther would understand from this that she had neither avoided, nor felt herself avoided.

'Ha-ha!' Stan laughed falsely. 'Out with your Italian boy friend? Does he take you to shows, or what?'

'Yes, we like to see plays at some of the little theatres. They do some interesting things.' She looked at the back of Esther's head, and then at Stan's, nervously. The atmosphere seemed to ring as it does when high-tension cables scream above a lonely road.

Stan laughed again, apparently finding nothing to say on the subject of little theatres; instead, he put added concentration into his driving, gesturing with careful concern, indicating to his passengers that he was occupied, that he had withdrawn from their company.

'You're lucky.' Esther's voice shocked the silence. 'I seldom have the pleasure of my husband's company at night until it's much too late to think of going out.'

No one spoke.

'Of course I don't ask where he has been. I know he's a very busy man, an important man, Rachel,' she said, involving the girl more by speaking her name. 'I know that I should be glad to sit by myself day and night, waiting for him to come home.'

There was another silence until Stan said, 'Haven't seen you down at the pool lately, Rae?'

Before she could answer, Esther cut in coldly, 'You haven't been there yourself, unless I am mistaken. He has rather a poor memory,' she called over her shoulder. 'You must excuse him.'

'We usually go to one of the beaches. I haven't been to the pool for a long time,' Rachel said, hoping that the accuracy of the guess would atone for the exposure. But she wondered immediately why she should care about protecting Stan. Of all the people she knew he seemed least in need, and least deserving, of help. Then she saw that it was Esther she was trying to defend, that it was fear of seeing Esther diminished that made her refuse to act as a sounding board for her pitiful retaliation. Whatever should be said between them, *this* was not right.

Esther shrank with shame at the sound of her own voice, but at the same time the desire that compelled her to speak flourished with angry joy. Too many nights of silent fear and humiliation had given birth to this voice; she was unable to silence it. Gathering sustenance from the memories of nights spent listening for Stan's footsteps, of hours spent wondering whether he would be raving, or kind, as he still could be, this voice overruled all others. But now, as it sometimes did, the violated centre hinted at rebellion; the sensation of it surged in her chest, lighting momentary panic.

Rachel started to tell a long story about the latest mishap at the office. A bundle of books had been mislaid. She was so depressed by strain and pity that the words had little meaning for her, and could have none, she knew, for Esther and Stan. But she gabbled on, mouthing inanities, her eyes flickering from one to the other.

'It isn't sensible to make such a commotion, because if the books are lost, the firm is insured, and in a few weeks Mr Butler will have forgotten all about this and be worrying about some new disaster. We have them regularly.' Her voice faded.

'Mmm. Too bad,' said Stan, who had been listening with the same exaggerated attention that he had previously given to his driving. Esther had been successfully silenced, and sat quiet until, at last, Rachel left the car and went into the office building.

With a sigh of relief she decided that it was much easier to endure Mr Butler's erratic temper than the threatening attention, the complex, unhappy emotions left behind in the car.

She wondered why it should be so as the automatic lift carried her, its only passenger, silently up the chill, narrow shaft.

Perhaps because Mr Butler's is avoidable. A reasonable man would be calm about the constant crises of business life. But Esther and Stan—I don't know—from what I've seen neither of them is reasonable, but the thing is: would it matter if they were? Would they still behave as they did just now?

She let herself into the cloakroom and combed her hair in front of the long mirror. Again she thought, I don't know, putting herself off because for a moment she was too interested in a new idea, almost too shocked by it, to answer. Reason would make no difference.

So it isn't omnipotent when feeling is involved? But why should it be, invariably? Surely one is as valuable as the other, and has its allotted moment of supremacy in any situation? Perhaps a perpetual balance...?

No. Balance and stalemate seemed synonymous.

But why do I feel that I've just realised that? I knew when I was being organised by Mrs Maitland that I often looked stupid but it felt right, so I didn't care. Anyway there was reason in it...But those two...

A young voice called, 'Hi! You're early. I thought I'd be first.'

Rachel whirled round. 'Oh, Stella! Yes, some people gave me a lift.' And thoughts of reason and feeling gave way to a discussion of Mr Butler's lack of both.

Coming down from the office at one o'clock the lift was crammed with girls. Tall girls and short, mostly slim, mostly pretty, all fresh and nicely dressed. They all read the weekly articles in the women's magazines which exhorted them to scrupulous cleanliness, smartness, spick-and-spanness. They all drank milk and orange juice, eschewed sweets and pastries. They lived for the evenings and the long weekends spent in the sun and air.

On this weekday they stood in the lift, warm bare arms touching, white gloves on, bags clutched, high-heeled feet eager to be out and off down the street to the store where, in imagination, they were already considering the jewel-coloured net, the golden sandals, the lipsticks, the dozens of such necessities that burnt their salaries. If there was time when they returned to the office they might eat a smooth, green-skinned Granny Smith's apple and a salad sandwich, but if not, there was the brown-paper parcel in the bottom drawer of the desk, the sight of which at intervals all afternoon more than compensated.

The folding doors crashed open and they clattered along the fawn-and-white marbled corridor.

'Are you coming with me till I change these shoes?' Stella asked, as she and Rachel stood side by side in the doorway, watching the hurrying crowds.

Rachel thought not. She felt hungry and the idea of standing by while Stella waited to be served, and then explained to some disenchanted woman that the shoes hurt her and couldn't be the right size, did not appeal. She said so, and Stella went off, justly agreeing that it wasn't much of a way of spending lunchtime.

As Rachel shook off her office thoughts and prepared to launch herself into the street, Mrs Maitland came hurrying up, out of breath, brilliant with pleasure and promise.

'I'm glad I got here in time, Rae. I had to come in to do some shopping and I thought we'd have lunch together—unless you've planned something else.'

No, oh no, there was nothing else. Rachel felt her heart beating gaily at the unexpectedness of her luck as she smiled into Laura's eyes.

'What about Luigi, though? I thought you might be going with him?'

'He has this administrative job helping Mr Butler, now. I don't see him very much during the day. He's often away.'

'But it's still going strong?' Laura persisted.

Put off by the inelegant expression, looking on

221

it as a kind of blasphemy, Rachel nevertheless had to say, 'Yes.'

It was clear to her that Mrs Maitland had not come to meet her to talk about Luigi, but she knew that it was her custom to talk to each person she met, first of all about themselves, or whatever she knew would interest them more: a harmless, even agreeable, social habit viewed by Rachel, when turned on her, with stark dislike. But then, to Rachel—unable to disentangle tact from hypocrisy, frailty from deliberate fraud—all of Laura's social habits were reprehensible.

Overcome with gloom at being treated to her most conventional approach she now put one foot in front of the other and saw nothing.

'Did you notice how well he and Bill got on the other night at dinner?' Laura said. 'Did you know that you two are to be our first weekend visitors when the house is finished? They fixed it up between them.'

'No! I didn't know that. He must have forgotten to tell me.'

'We both liked him very much.'

'Did you?'

Rachel's determination to believe that this was conventional small talk dissolved. Wanting confirmation of Laura's approval, she could not restrain the eager turn of her head.

They pushed through the revolving door of the restaurant and a minute later looked at the menu.

'Have something interesting,' Laura said. 'It's my party.'

Eyeing them coldly, the waitress wrote on her pad and moved on to the next table.

'Well, now...' Laura removed her gloves, fixed a kindly, tolerant gaze on Rachel and leaned forward. She was about to speak when the girl opened her handbag. Her expression changed.

'That's new, isn't it, Rae?'

'Yes, do you like it? I bought it in a place in the Imperial Arcade.'

'It's gorgeous. It's just reminded me: that's something else I'll have to put on my shopping list.'

The square, low-ceilinged room was cool, full of pale light, subdued voices. The tables were all occupied, mostly by women, and the walls were lined with mirrors so cut that Rachel, as she sat in her corner seat, looked down a long passage of her reflected face, scores of images of her face, diminishing, but ending where? Laura scanned the walls for acquaintances and lit a cigarette.

Suddenly she said, 'I saw you leaving with the Petersons this morning.'

'Yes. They had to be in town early.'

'I haven't seen much of them lately, have you?' Laura looked at her curiously through a cloud of smoke.

'No.'

The waitress brought their order. After she left they

223

were silent, looking at the formidable dish of lobster mayonnaise, doubting one another.

Grinding her cigarette out, Laura leaned forward again. In a low voice she said, 'I can trust you, can't I, Rae? You won't repeat it if I tell you something in confidence?'

Uneasily Rachel shook her head. Jealous curiosity and a resolution to defend Laura's integrity from herself combined to make her face unreadable.

Laura looked at her sharply. 'You're sure?'

Rachel shook her head again. Her face was young and blank. She began to eat.

'Well,' Laura said, a trifle let down, 'the other day I was at Cassie Roberts'—you know Cass, don't you?—and guess what I found out? Who do you think I saw? It'll floor you, I can tell you. I nearly had a stroke!' She raised her eyebrows, lowered her voice, 'Stan Peterson and his girl friend. Same block of flats. She lives next to Cass. There's a piece of news to open your eyes. Not that it's really surprising, I suppose; he's a pretty low type. But what do you think of it?'

Rachel's gaze rested on her for an instant. She chewed stolidly at a piece of lobster. Chewing the last mouthful seemed suddenly to have become a great effort, requiring much patience, time. 'I don't know. It's awful,' she said at length, without expression.

Really, Laura thought, she's very unsophisticated. Perhaps I shouldn't have told her. She ate for a few

224

moments without speaking, then she said, 'You didn't know anything about it?'

They exchanged a glance.

'No. Well. I've been wondering what I should do about it. It's had me worried all week. You know, we're about the only women friends Esther has apart from that stepmother and sister-in-law that she doesn't see very often. I don't know if it wouldn't be better to come from me now, than from someone else when it's too late to do anything about it. You can't carry on like that without the whole world finding out. He's a fool.'

A slight tense frown appeared on Rachel's forehead as her mind moved reluctantly to face what she already knew.

'You mean...you're going to tell her?'

Laura looked at her carefully, seemed struck by what she saw, and put down her knife and fork. She rested her arms on the table more, it might have been thought, for moral, than physical support.

'Yes, I think I am. Rae, why don't you try to be a bit kinder? Why do you always sit in judgement? This is a real problem—I can't dodge it. I have to do what I think is right. I don't want to hurt anyone. Has it occurred to you that I might as easily be right as you?'

Rachel went cold, could not lift her eyes, could not move.

'Sometimes I wonder what you really do think of me. You've got very high standards for me, haven't you? And you're afraid I can't come up to them.'

After another silence Laura moved her hands, picked up her knife and fork. She looked at her plate without attention. When eventually Rachel flashed a look at her, she had about her an air so withdrawn and vulnerable, so undoubtedly genuine, that Rachel's youthful arrogance crashed in panic.

Desolately she pushed some food about on her plate. She brought out at last, 'No, I only meant *I* wouldn't like to tell Esther.'

'You don't have to explain to me. I know exactly what you thought.'

After a suffocating pause, Rachel said again, head lowered, 'I only meant *I* wouldn't like to tell her.'

Laura took a deep breath. Glancing at the crowded room she frowned and said, with an assumption of briskness, 'No, that would hardly do. You're just a young girl. You can't know how it feels to a woman to know that her man has gone to someone else. It isn't a job that anyone can look forward to—even me.'

She stopped, put aside with her last words the pretence of indifference. 'Look up. Look at me, Rae. That's right. This has given you a shock. You're not used to the idea of these things happening, are you? But that's not the thing, is it? You think I'll enjoy telling Esther. That's what's wrong with you, isn't it?'

'No!' Glassily Rachel looked at her. 'Oh, no, I don't. That wasn't what…I didn't mean…'

'No?' said Laura lightly. She was silent for a time, then she added, 'I hope not, Rae...Perhaps, now, *I've* been unkind. You made me angry, though.'

Neither seeming to know after this whether she was the forgiven or the forgiver, both leaned back rather meekly from the table while the waitress clashed dishes over them and stared at herself in the mirrored walls.

When they were alone again Laura said, 'The truth is, I really believe Esther's better to know. I'm afraid she cares for him, poor girl. I know what it'll mean. I know how I'd feel if it were Bill. I couldn't go on.'

'Then mightn't it be better to leave it? I mean—it might not have been what you thought. Or it mightn't last. She might be just a friend—the woman you saw.'

The mask of gravity held, broke, and Laura smiled. 'Do you really think I wouldn't know the difference? Do you?'

Rachel dropped her eyes, despising herself—for with Esther's problem to be thought of it was no time to enjoy herself—but feeling altogether vanquished by the news, Laura's decision, the maternal warmth of her face and voice. She could not not smile.

'Ah, darling,' Laura laughed a little. 'If you'd seen the blonde hair and the bust, you wouldn't have doubted either.'

Trying to find her independence, Rachel thought that blonde hair, even dyed, was no crime. And as for busts, after all...

227

Drawn away by some thought, Laura was silent. She had no intention of telling Rachel that she and Bill had actually quarrelled about this—quarrelled for the first since she couldn't remember when. Not badly. Like her, he had been sorry for Esther. Now he agreed that she should be told, but days had passed and Laura had done nothing. Very soon, though, she would have to speak.

Rachel opened her mouth to ask about Anabel. She felt helpless to persuade Laura to change her mind; doubted the rightness of her own instinct. It might be a kind of cowardice on her part. She concluded that she would achieve not less, perhaps more, by allowing the Petersons to be forgotten. But Laura smiled at her.

'Cheer up! Eat up that ice-cream and let's get out of here, like a good girl. And don't look so guilty. This is all very sad for Esther, but it's not *our* fault.'

Getting busy with her spoon, Rachel cheered up. 'Where's Anabel today? Auntie Barbie's? I never get a chance to see her any more and she *had* to be sleepy the other night...'

CHAPTER TWENTY-TWO

The sun was going down when Marion Prescott lifted the sprinkler and carried it to a dry patch of grass. Esther stood by the garden tap and turned it on again when her stepmother had moved out of the way. Trailing back across the lawn she returned to the seat under the jacaranda tree where she had been sitting in the sun all afternoon. Marion joined her, noticing again with concern the extreme thinness of Esther's face and arms, her shadowed eyes. She thought she had never seemed less approachable.

Aloud she said: 'David and Clem should be home soon, and Hector and Angela promised not to be late.'

Esther half-turned her head to show that she had heard. 'It's so quiet here after town,' she said at last. 'I miss the garden.' Raising her arm she pointed to an old gum tree, miraculously spared when the site was cleared for building years before. 'I used to have a swing on that tree when I was small.'

'I know. When Phillip and I came to visit your father—oh, how many years ago, twenty-five?—we often saw you there on Sunday afternoons. Do you remember him at all?'

'Your brother Phillip? Yes. He was nice. He used to tell me stories.'

'He liked children.'

A family of small birds hopped and fluttered across the lawn until they came within range of the light spray of water thrown by the sprinkler. Esther followed their progress, watched them splash and play and startle one another and fly away a minute or so later.

'We—Stan and I—had thought of a house with a garden,' she said, leaning forward to pick up a twig.

'I know, Esther.'

'David told you?'

'Do you mind?'

'No.' Her voice was expressionless. She peeled the rough bark from the stick with restless fingers.

The last rays of the sun lit her face, exposing the tightness of the skin on her cheekbones, the hollowed planes; lit the garden with a strange, pink radiance so that the full-blown roses waving in the evening breeze shone in momentary glory like planets amongst the other flowers.

230

Noticing the colour in the sky, Esther said mechanically, 'Another hot day tomorrow.' She dropped the clean, creamy twig to the ground and turned suddenly to Marion. 'I wish I hadn't come today. Oh, I wanted to see you, Marion, but I can't wait. I can't see them all. I'll have to go. You'll make excuses for me, won't you? There's nothing I could say to them. Please.' She half-started from the seat, in a fever to be gone, but Marion, alarmed by the panic in her eyes, restrained her with a touch of her hand.

'Of course,' she said calmly, 'you must go if you want to. They'll be disappointed, but that won't do them any harm. I'm selfish—I've seen you, so I can say that. But perhaps we all tried to hurry this meeting too much. It's our fault.' She looked round the garden, at a loss. The light was fading quickly. 'They're all so fond of you.'

'Fond?'

'They are afraid of losing you altogether,' Marion said.

'Are they? I wonder why. I suppose because they feel they should be. It's more likely that they feel I'm an embarrassment. But they're kind, aren't they? They're nice. I don't know.'

Marion was silent.

Esther said, 'I'll go now—by the back lane.'

She stood up and Marion walked with her round the side of the house to the small lattice gate. Esther

231

could smell the wet grass and the sun-dried hedge whose leaves she had idly plucked and pleated years before.

'I'm sorry to go like this, Marion. Please forgive me. It isn't that I'm trying to hide anything from them; they know more about our affairs than I do myself I've no doubt—men are so thorough. But there's nothing to say now. No point...'

'In a few weeks it may seem different to you,' Marion said, affecting to believe what she did not.

'I don't think so. You must see how it is,' she said in a flat, exhausted voice.

In the brief twilight of luminous blue both women found it easier to speak than during the brilliant afternoon, and Marion asked, 'May I come to see you soon?'

'Yes, of course, any afternoon.' The response was swift and polite, but a moment later she touched her stepmother's hand and said, 'I'd really like you to.' Then, again speaking rapidly, as if hastening away from her own thoughts, she said, 'What exactly did David tell you, Marion?'

Marion stirred. 'Why make yourself more unhappy, Esther? It would be better to leave it. I'd rather.'

'I suppose you're right,' she said, gazing unseeing at the ground. 'I wish David's principles had not been so high. Stan never hurts anyone but himself with all his business dealings. He's never been in trouble. He's never robbed anyone. He just isn't David, that's all. He hasn't had time for principles.'

'David meant well, I know. He was thinking of you.'

Opening the gate, Esther walked slowly into the lane. 'It isn't really enough, is it? Meaning well. Don't let them discuss—anything tonight, will you?'

They embraced and she was gone, past the high fences and the overhanging trees, the solid mansions' leafy gardens and lighted windows.

When Marion Prescott said that Esther had not waited to see them, Hector went immediately to the telephone, but there was no reply from her number.

'She won't be there yet,' David said. 'I think I'll drive over and catch her before she goes in. I'll bring her back.'

Clem and Marion both said, 'No!' And Clem went on, 'I don't think so, David. We should leave her alone. It's what she wants and it's probably the best thing we can do for her. We should accept it. Give her a few more weeks.'

Hector could see that Angela was annoyed: they had cancelled another dinner engagement to come this evening, but his feeling of dismay sprang from a deeper cause than his wife's surface annoyance. She was a pretty woman who thought herself beautiful. Several times she had been on the short list of the year's best-dressed women: apart from that she was very similar to most of her friends. Hector knew that since the day he had confided to her the substance of David's interview with Peterson, Angela had set about a reconstruction of her opinion of his sister. A certain unadmitted respect turned to pity, this gave way to disdain, and that again to irritation; lastly came rancour, and fear that she and Hector might be involved in some way in a scandal.

Hector lit a cigarette and looked across at her as she sat twirling the thin stem of her glass between her fingers, shooting him glances of exasperation and reproach. He sighed imperceptibly.

Clem was Marion's ally this evening as on other occasions. Feeling her appeal he roused himself to draw his brothers into general conversation. When the talk turned to politics even Angela dropped her sulky pose. She had a second cousin who was a Liberal MP and, she said, rather a sweet thing. He would make a handsome Prime Minister.

Marion, relieved to see that David no longer slumped in his chair, listened and interposed a comment now and then.

The men, discussing war, looked up, startled, and then smiled slowly when she said, 'So stimulating—war. You don't think that there's a moral value in pacificism—taken to its furthest extremes—that might have an equally strong effect?'

'Hardly,' David smiled. 'Everyone believes in the pacifist ideal—up to a point, and especially women—but no one practises it, and for very good reasons. I wonder if you do realise all that it would imply?'

'That's a bit tough, isn't it?' Clem rebuked him mildly, looking from one to the other. 'If he understood you at all, Marion, he would know that you are not a woman to make such a statement without knowing what you mean.'

'Thank you, Clem. I could defend myself, but I think I won't. I doubt if David is open to persuasion.'

'Perhaps not. But I apologise,' David said. 'You surprised me. I respect your opinion on all kinds of things, Marion, but you haven't often come out with anything that's surprised me as much as this.'

She smiled at him as if she could believe this.

'What do you suppose Stan Peterson was doing during the war?' Angela murmured.

Hector put his glass on the table by his side. 'I envy you two your cellar.'

'Cellar!' David exclaimed. 'You know very well that it's a small cupboard—all too small. However,' he admitted, 'it has its beauties.'

As Clem refilled the glasses Marion thought that whatever were the merits of the liquid he poured, the effect had been a blessed loosening of tension. There had been forgetfulness of guilt on David's part, regret on Hector's; Angela was more animated; Clem looked less tired, while she herself, remembering Esther, hoped with more hope that a lapse of time would end misunderstandings.

'Angela, dear, and boys,' she said, when Clem had

finished, 'I don't want to rush you through to the dining room, but you know Mrs Ramsay. I don't know what will happen if we allow her special efforts for us to wither in front of her eyes...'

As they left the room, carrying their glasses carefully, smiling and relaxed, Esther arrived at the front door of her flat.

It seemed to her that she had been hailed by at least six people on the way upstairs, and now, in sight of peace, here was Rachel standing dumbly at the door waiting for her; standing alone in the long, quiet passageway, turning anxious eyes on her.

Hiding her instinctive withdrawal, resignedly holding herself firm, she said coolly, 'Hello, Rachel. Were you coming to see me?' She fitted the key in the lock.

'Yes. I'd just rung the bell when I heard you coming upstairs. I saw the garage was empty and I thought I'd come up. I...'

'Then come in,' Esther said, holding the door open for her. 'Stan probably won't be home for hours.'

Her tone was not uncordial, but still Rachel hesitated in the doorway. 'I only meant to stay for a little while,' she said awkwardly, 'but you've been out...If you're tired or anything I'll just go...'

There was a silence and Rachel's embarrassment increased; she felt enormous with embarrassment. Esther repeated quietly, 'Come in,' and Rachel went forward, walking gingerly on the balls of her feet, as if by treading lightly and noiselessly she might give less offence.

Esther waved her through to the sitting room while she went to change her clothes. She called that there were some American magazines on the little table or somewhere in the room, and would she like to amuse herself with them for five minutes.

Obediently taking the suggestion as an order, Rachel picked up one and began to flip the pages over. Smooth glossy paper. A three-decker cake thick with chocolate icing, brightly yellow and brown, loomed three-dimensionally for a second and was overturned. All the best people wear these watches, smoke these cigarettes, wear these furs, clean their houses with these vacuum cleaners...

Faster and faster her hand turned the pages and then it stopped altogether. She had to think. It was wasted effort, time, to pretend when there was no one to deceive. She had to think. Her heart was pounding with alarm as she asked herself yet again how she was to prevent Esther from listening to Mrs Maitland. It was for this reason that she had come tonight, but now that she was here nothing seemed possible. Hopelessly she thought that Laura's silence was the only solution, and she knew that she could achieve nothing there.

Behind her, venetian blinds which had been lowered earlier in the day against the sun rocked unevenly in the wind and tapped on the window frame. Rachel jerked her head at the noise, and as she did she thought of Stan and her heart leapt. Could she warn him? Catch him before he came in? Face him? Tell him? She knew that she could not. Hearing Esther's footsteps in the hall she hastily reopened the magazine.

They both smiled formally and started a scrappy conversation while Esther cooked an egg and made some coffee. She said that she thought Pauline and Bob looked well after their holiday; she had called in to see them in the morning. Stan wanted to have a game with Bob on Saturday if he wasn't booked up. He would go down to ask him tonight sometime. There was a new dress on the bed that Rachel might like to see. Was she sure she wouldn't have anything to eat or drink? Oh. If she had finished dinner as recently as that...

Their eyes met just as often as politeness made necessary and Rachel, stricken by a thought that only her perturbation had excluded for so long, began to find even these few encounters unbearable.

What if she seemed like a kind of blackmailer, coming up without being asked—a thing she'd never done before—as if she wanted to see what was going on, sure that she wouldn't be turned out because of what she'd seen and heard that night? What if that was what Esther thought?

Common sense said in its literal voice that a single call, several weeks after the event, scarcely amounted to spying or any kind of blackmail. And where was the benefit to her? What was the payment? She wasn't a heart-eater. A heart-eater? No, but still...

When Esther asked about Luigi—How was he? How had his family settled down?—Rachel was too unnerved to feel at all outraged that he should be the subject of a perfunctory inquiry. She knew that this was the end, too. No more could be said. His name came as her dismissal. The inquiry asked, Esther's duty was done.

'I'd better go,' she said shrilly. 'I only meant to stay for a few minutes.'

Her persistence in staying, the futility of intentions—these, and Esther's quiet dignity—cut into the girl's conscience. To Rachel it seemed now that all the trust of the world was to be betrayed, that some kind of innocence, to which she could not aspire, was to be shattered. She felt accused of all things bad. She was ashamed for herself and Laura, for Stan and the woman, whoever she was.

She turned to go but Esther stopped her. 'I didn't mean to be unpleasant in the car, Rachel, or to—'

'You weren't.'

'I think I was, but I'm sorry. I've been on edge— not feeling well—but it's no excuse. I hoped you would understand. And poor Stan...'

Rachel nodded vigorously at the floor. They walked slowly to the door.

'Are you going to be busy on Saturday?'

'I'm meeting Luigi at one. I'm not doing anything in the morning, though.'

'That was what I meant, really. I wondered if you'd like to come for a swim while Stan's playing golf? Don't say yes unless you'd like to...Along to the pool.'

'But I *would* like to,' Rachel smiled, and relinquishing all responsibility, prayed that Laura would change her mind. 'What time should I be ready?'

Esther frowned suddenly and gave an exclamation. 'Oh! I'd forgotten. Laura phoned today and asked me down on Saturday morning for coffee.'

Once again Rachel was conscious of the beating of her heart. 'Phoned?' she echoed. So it's all arranged. Fixed.

'Yes. I am sorry.' Esther smiled a little at Rachel's expression and thought how young she was.

'Forget it!' she said with a nervous, reckless laugh. 'Don't go! She'll only want to gossip and you don't enjoy it much, do you?'

'I don't see how I can get out of it now. I should have remembered before I spoke. I am sorry, pet. Perhaps *next* week? What do you say? And I won't make any more appointments to gossip with Laura till we've fixed it?' She looked at Rachel kindly, her tone softening as she saw how strangely crestfallen she seemed.

On the stairs Rachel passed Stan. She hardly noticed him until he said, 'If you weren't so gloomy you wouldn't be a bad-looking girl.'

Then, automatically, she stretched her mouth, but he had gone, racing upstairs two at a time. The door banged and he was home. Home early.

'Est?...Est?' he shouted and she went to meet him, hearing something in his voice that made her wonder, doubt. How are we now? Where do we stand?

She stopped before she reached him. 'Hello?' She waited to see if she had been mistaken. 'Washing up,' she said, holding her rubber-gloved hands towards him.

'Hello, pet,' he said, and found that he could not control his voice. They looked at each other for a long time.

Stan said, 'It lasted too long, didn't it, Est? Didn't it, baby?' He drew her into his arms with a suppressed groan. 'What was it all about? Do you know? It's been hell, hasn't it? Why do we do these things to ourselves?'

Why they should have come together now without words or effort when other agonisingly rehearsed scenes had only hardened the strain between them, she did not know. But even as she felt his hands and mouth, part of her mind took up his question, recoiling, almost fearful that he could ask it. Took up his question, but for half a second only, and then she closed her eyes.

That night after he left her she lay in the darkness falling in and out of sleep, consciousness ebbing, reaching a prescribed extremity and flowing back. It was late. The surrounding flats were silent; there was an occasional street scuffle, half mechanical, half human, but apart

241

from that—nothing. A small room, a silver moon caught in a silver mirror, two figures humped in two narrow beds, each conscious that the other was awake.

Even Stan sensed, though less acutely than Esther, the current that seemed to flow between them, but both missed the universal nature of the link in a way that the Maitlands, who called themselves an ordinary couple, did not. The Maitlands knew themselves to be of unusual excellence as partners, gave themselves first place on the list of happy marriages, but allowed that there might be others, different in degree perhaps, but not in kind. Esther saw herself and Stan as unique; their union losing nothing for being dangerous and dark at times; and Stan walked his own mind, a distorted giant, and viewed his wife, his closest tie, through the same untruthful glass.

Now, he allowed his thoughts to drift to Esther with satisfaction and a powerful beating of his heart, with some regret, with humility and a few aspirations. Est was very happy now, he thought, and so was he. The situation was under control. Comfortably swaddled in well being, he moved on to the new job that occupied most of his working hours. Another dollar job. Those damned restrictions, he murmured lovingly. Oh, those restrictions. There was a definite warmth in his veins when he thought of them. The shadows of his associates on the job moved before his eyes; faces and names and voices that knew when to be discreet; fellows who could be found in any one of half a dozen pubs, who lived nowhere, with no one, and had no lives but the one he saw. That was the proper way, too. Not like the old days when they were all pals on and off duty. But still good boys, he thought. All good boys as long as you watched them.

And Vi, he thought after a while. Good old Vi. He would see her at the weekend. He was getting sleepy again, sinking, drifting, and the thought of Vi went down to sleep with him, sucked down into his mind like a broken ship to the seabed. He slept.

Esther knew at once. She turned on the pillows and looked across the room but his face was in shadow. She heard his steady breathing. She lay with one arm trailing over the edge of the low divan and her fingers, uncurling, stretched out towards him as she looked, as if to call him back to consciousness.

Circumstance had bent her head, compelled her to see what she would not. Unwilling, she had acquiesced and agreed to see as many facts as she must: facts which left her not unhopeful, which brought with them a new and adult arrangement of beliefs. They brought, too, a tightening of her obsessive passion.

I know him better than he knows himself, she thought. These bad weeks are over, and already he has forgotten them. These nights and nights that made me want to die—a blank to him. Poor Stan—lucky Stan. But who could want him to remember?

She knew that if he had gone back to look for causes he would have blamed David, told her to think of their ruined plans. The miserable series of personal disasters that had followed their meeting could be attributed only to David. It would seem natural and manly to Stan that he should have reacted as he had, drinking and raging until stomach and brain rebelled.

She had come to see Stan's personality as one so precariously balanced on his desperate need for universal admiration, that criticism, however just, from anyone he deemed superior, plunged him from normality to a state where pride was burned and thought and feeling ran molten. After long ages and a period of forgetfulness he came back, and all was as it had been before.

Half sleeping, she looked across at him again and was content. She felt that whatever either of them was, with the help of the other, all would be well.

CHAPTER TWENTY-THREE

Heavy pounding rain fell from a summer sky that had lately been a harsh bright blue; now thick clouds chugged and swirled in the low darkness. The hollow crack of rolling thunder was past, but the rain still pelted down, a solid wall of water.

Though the air inside was warm and sticky, Laura shivered suddenly in a draught and sent Anabel to fetch a cardigan for her. Visibility ended within a few feet of the window. She stared, shivered again, and clasped her arms across her bosom.

Anabel came back, dropped the soft yellow thing at her mother's feet and turned a neat somersault. She thought about repeating her success and was preparing, after natural deliberation, to stand on her head, when Laura swooped on her unexpectedly from behind and lifted her in the air. She shrieked with annoyance, but such was her delight in change that she withheld a more coherent protest until she saw what was to happen. The next minute she was downstairs, installed in the Demsters' flat with Teddy and a few of her old books. Remembering, then, that she had been badly treated, Anabel pouted resentfully at her mother and Pauline Demster.

Mrs Demster hoped rather worriedly that she would be able to cope with her, and wished Rachel had not chosen this morning to fling herself out of the place looking so mysterious and dramatic. She could have amused Anabel perfectly.

'It's terribly kind of you,' Laura was saying. 'I wouldn't have bothered you on a Saturday morning and especially with Rae not here, but I've got some rather important business to talk over with a friend, and I felt I should have her out of the way.' She lowered her voice and glanced down at Anabel, hoping she had not heard.

'I'm sure we'll get on very well,' Mrs Demster said, thinking as she spoke how charming Laura was. It was not surprising that Rachel had been so fond of her.

Her pale face unusually animated, she tried to keep Laura by talking about Rachel and Luigi: she tried to be charming, and her voice leapt and trilled, her hands waved. She saw failure coming and she tried a little harder, but the bubbling excitement drained slowly

246

away. She was keeping Mrs Maitland when she wanted to go.

Disappointed, Pauline Demster knelt on the floor and played with Anabel for a few minutes before returning to the kitchen.

As she ran back upstairs Laura's eyes grew small and their lustre was extinguished. That she exercised her gifts at some cost to herself was a truth that she accepted, seeing her pain as a payment to the gods who had blessed her. The strain was hardest when, as had happened this morning, she used herself entirely against her will. With the middle-aged, the unsmart, the uncomplicated, the clever, or with those who surrendered to her too easily, she was quickly and profoundly bored; bored until she felt her chest wasted, powdery and sore with it; bored until she almost ceased to breathe. She could not forgive them. The core of glamorous heat in her was a sacred thing—its wastage or misuse a sin, not a payment. Minutes of her life were eaten every day by clayey mortals. She was preyed on. Sitting in a straight-backed chair by the window she lit a cigarette and noticed that the rain had stopped and the sky was clearing. Five minutes passed, and some ash fell on the thin silk of her skirt. She brushed it away with a slow abstracted movement. I'd want to know if it was Bill, she thought defensively, touching the wooden arm of her chair with superstitious dread. I'd want to know, she thought again, insisting.

Poor girl, I'm afraid she really loves him, she thought, and all at once her eyes were wet. This isn't the first time this has happened, she told herself. You've seen it often enough before. Better to know and do something about it, than have it come up months hence when it's gone on so long that nothing can help.

Drearily she repeated what she had said to Rachel. It still seemed true, but she was depressed by what she was about to do. Her responsive, sympathetic heart ached.

She finished her cigarette, rose, smoothed her skirt, looked out of the window, prodded the cushion back into shape, went to the kitchen where the percolator was bubbling and switched it off. There was a knock at the door while she was there, and when she called, Esther answered and came in.

In spite of acute apprehension over the words that she must inevitably say, Laura found that half an hour passed easily over coffee and cigarettes. They shuffled through a batch of new photographs of Anabel, and talked about possible designs for some dresses for her. Laura told about her latest party, and about a friend she had made. A married woman whose husband Bill had known for ages. Marvellous skin, and what hair, and teeth! Really, she was a dream, and the thing was she didn't know it. Just didn't notice how beautiful she was.

The room swam with rain-wet sunshine, and Esther, facing the windows, half-closed her eyes against it. Laura's voice went on and on, deep, mellow.

Esther thought about peaches. She would buy some. And what else? Cheese, gherkins, perhaps. It was so long since she and Stan had had meals together that she had almost forgotten how to shop and cook. But they would be out tonight, and out all day tomorrow, so she needn't worry much about food until Monday... But Laura had stopped speaking, so Esther focused her eyes on her again and smiled.

'We're driving to the mountains for the day, tomorrow,' she began, feeling it was time for a contribution. 'We don't—like—the South...' She stopped slowly, by degrees, braked, as it were, by the look on Laura's face.

'Esther! I shouldn't have waited so long. I asked you down this morning for a particular reason. But I suppose when it came to the point I hardly knew how to go about it...'

Esther sat forward on the sofa and looked down at her hands, saw the sun glittering on the diamonds on her fingers. She looked back at Laura. 'Oh? What is it?'

And then Laura was speaking '...in the block on the corner of Baker and Trident Streets...a woman, a Mrs Rogers, a barmaid...didn't see very much, but... thought you should know...hated to tell you, but...'

Listen to what she's saying, Esther told herself with frozen calm. Remember it and think about it later. The sentences filed themselves in her mind, but their content was so unexpected, so unlikely, and so quaintly put that she could listen almost indifferently. And Laura's expression was absurd.

She has seen Stan with one of those making-up women...she works for him, of course, but Laura doesn't know that. She might have seen him talking to ten different women...How surprised she would have been—ten girl friends!

She could have laughed, but somehow before the shape and sound reached her lips she changed her mind, and the fluttering inner giggles went cold. Fleeting depression was succeeded by an anger that left her weak.

That Laura should talk to *her*—tell her a story like this about Stan—talk to her about *him*—watch her face—wait to see her reaction to a story like this...

She was an imperial image, inscrutable. She lowered her eyelids. It was the first movement she had made: it was the only sign she gave that she had heard, and it touched Laura more than she could bear. Tears came to her eyes. She lifted her arms and shifted along the sofa.

'Darling,' she said, 'I didn't want...'

Evading the arms, Esther stood up. She cleared her throat for she wanted her voice to be steady, and it seemed a long time since she had spoken. Laura gazed up at her, curious and alarmed. The clear impersonality of the voice, when it came, frightened her.

'I'm sure you thought you were doing what was right in telling me this, Laura. But I'm afraid you've made a mistake. I know Mrs Rogers. She is one of

250

several women who do part-time work for my husband. He visits them all frequently. They often have to go to the factory with him to be shown how to assemble new work. I sometimes go with him.' She paused for a moment to get control of her breath; she was beginning to feel faint. 'I heard nothing in your story to suggest...' She stopped on a note infinitely remote and snubbing.

Laura sat stunned. Later, she was to try feverishly to recall that other morning and the little scene, to try to remember why she had been so convinced that the pair were lovers. But nothing more specific came to her mind than the tones of the voices, the expressions, caught for an instant, the slight scuffle in the doorway that she had suspected but not seen: these things, and an intuition that had never before been mistaken.

But now she sat incapable of thought. 'Oh, my God!' she said. 'My God!'

At last she struggled up from the sofa and stood in front of Esther. She tried to speak but she blushed instead—a slow blush that started at her waist and swept hotly over her arms and face.

'I don't know how to apologise to you, Esther. I can't apologise. I can only say that I saw what I told you—and I thought you should know about it. As God's my judge I meant it for the best. I really did.'

Esther's level gaze exposed her. She felt transparent. She seemed still to have to strain up to look at her. Even so, humiliated as she was, she smiled. She went

251

across the room, still speaking, hands trembling as she searched in her bag for cigarettes.

'You'll never know what an idiot I feel,' she confessed when she had at last lighted one. 'I deserve to, of course. I realise that. I've learnt a lesson.' She sat on the arm of a chair and looked straight at Esther. 'I don't know what you think of me. You probably won't believe me when I say I'm truly, sincerely, glad that I was wrong. I'm deeply relieved that it has ended like this, with me—poor old mug that I am—looking an ass, than the other way. Please...'

They looked at each other without speaking for a time, then Esther said neutrally, 'Have you told anyone else about this?'

It was impossible to lie to her. 'Bill—Rachel.'

'Bill and Rachel, I see.'

Laura got awkwardly to her feet. 'Won't you have a drink? I'm sure you could do with one as much as I could?...I don't want you to go away hating me. Come and sit down and let's...Stay just a minute...' The right words would not come. Esther refused and they parted: Laura to lie outstretched on her bed, a forearm across her eyes; Esther, to return upstairs.

She had said it so spontaneously, lied so well. 'I know Mrs Rogers.' But you don't, she said, falling limply into a chair, immediately standing up again. She pressed her hands together and took a few slow steps; she trod a small wavering circle. All normal speed

252

of thought and action had dropped from her: the life-sustaining functions of her body seemed to work with sick, spasmodic rhythm.

It wasn't true, but it had been said. She didn't believe it; neither did Laura now, and yet she must have been sure. She must have seen more than Stan simply talking to a strange woman, or else why should she think…?

I'd have known, she thought with fierce pride. I'd have known if he'd had another woman.

But her mouth trembled and she covered it with her hands. She closed her eyes. She moved her hands over her ears and stood with her head bent.

Alight with panic, her eyes started open; her hands fell. Had she cried out? Surely not, and yet, if she refrained from screaming, from beating herself against the wall, how much more surprising.

Languidly she moved over to the mirror and stared at the blank-eyed face that turned itself from side to side as if to penetrate a veil of fog. She turned away and said in a small, dry whisper, 'Because I know—I know he wouldn't do that to me.'

She saw the past weeks again as if they lay spread out on a page on her knee, and it seemed that all the sadness and trouble there had been inevitable. It was Stan and it had had to be. But it was over: they had passed that point. They were tired; they wanted one another, a smooth sea.

How can I wonder? How could I stand here if I

really wondered? Because Stan's all...And only last night he said...only last night...

She gave a little moan and closed her eyes. She rocked slowly backwards and forwards in an effort to silence her thoughts, to hold off the eerie hollowness, the fear and occupation that swung behind her head like threatening madness.

Sinking to her knees, she crouched in the narrow space between wall and chair, as small as she could be, hiding from tongues and eyes, from Stan and herself, consoled by arms and legs, warm skin, all parts of herself.

Dinner and dancing at Zito's, and the sensuous music of the tango, beating sharply then drawing out, lengthening on a note of wailing sweetness. The tables were packed with the people who had been there that other night: the same youthful beauties blooming under concealed lighting, kept alive by air-conditioning, served by waiters who moved silently on ball-bearing feet.

Sometimes the closeness of the other dancers, the accidental touch of skin, the cold eye of a stranger, the artificial gaiety of acquaintances made her want to swoon with horror. The unreality of attitudes, values, setting, seemed suddenly revealed to her. She saw behind the wall of skin and bone that was each face to the animal that lived behind the eyes, to the cruel pathetic creature that lived alone from birth to death.

She would endure her knowledge, dance with it while Stan held her, and then look up to find him smiling at her with cheerful confidence, or grinning across the table at her for her lost expression, brown eyes narrowed with amusement. 'What's up?' he would say quietly, still smiling, breathing with steady reassuring masculinity, making her fears recede.

This evening, while he kept his own glass full, he rarely touched it, but said, each time he lifted the bottle for Esther, 'No, I'm okay. Still got some. Do you good though, pet. Loosen you up.'

Now he was asking, 'What would you think about a trip to America next year—or maybe England? Huh?'

He looked at her bare tanned shoulders and arms, the sheer stiff black material of her dress, the diamonds swinging from her ears and shining on her hands, the red-painted mouth and the smooth red nails and he covered one of her hands with his, protectively. He felt extraordinarily sentimental: it was as if the old mixture of passion and reverence had been renewed at the source, strengthened.

But he made no loving speeches: he was not a man for speeches. He simply squeezed her arm and said, 'Can't be a slave all my days, can I? Never see anything of you. It's time we did something like that, honey. Have some fun together, you know.' He spoke in the flat expressionless way he had, not always looking at her, not opening his mouth more than he could help, but

Esther could tell that he was excited by this new idea, and wanted her enthusiasm. But, she thought, next year.

Her fingers slid round her glass as she answered him. She heard her voice, watched herself smile, and drank some wine. The music went on and on; the clockwork figures on the small floor whirled dizzily. A woman lurched as she came back to her table and the young man with her went white. They left soon afterwards, the woman trailing behind saying plaintively, 'But Dickie, I don't *want* to go home. Dickie...Dickie! I don't *want*...'

It was late when Esther and Stan reached home. Unaccountably, the hours between departure and return had brought an alleviation of fear. Perhaps a decision she herself had taken early in the evening had helped; so had Stan's declaration of his plan to go abroad. And his unstrained attentiveness had served in a conclusive way to cement the holes in her trust, to confirm the rightness of her violent denial of Laura's story.

Quite suddenly she was convinced that her reaction had been right. And the sudden discharge of nervous tension decided her to tell him.

While she smoothed cold cream on her face, Stan was putting his suit away, finding his dressing gown, tying the cord around his waist. She wiped her face with tissues and after several hesitations began, 'Stan, I was down at Laura's today...' But he had gone into the bathroom. The shower was running.

The door opened. He called, 'Did you say something? I was just about under the shower.'

'No! No, I was singing.'

There was an astonished pause, then, 'Singing?' he said, and added with exaggerated politeness as he banged the door again, 'Pardon me!'

Thinking of what she had, in a moment of hysterical foolishness, so nearly done, Esther sat paralysed. Then she saw the image of herself caught in the glass—raised hands, tense mouth—and deliberately relaxed.

The moment of shock past, she thought that, after all, she had done no harm. Stan was making a happy commotion in the bathroom, whistling and bellowing. The night outside was clear and bright with stars. The room was homely—untidy, of course, because Stan was in and he always kicked the rugs out of place— but familiar and colourful. She leaned forward to smell the freesias that he had brought for her, and was completely reassured. Their scent was real, tangible. Stan was singing so loudly now that she was sure the McCarthys next door would start to bang on the wall.

She lifted her hairbrush and began to do her hair. Monday lay in cast-iron bands: around it were high fences and warning signs.

It was Sunday and they were in the car early, driving through long miles of suburbs before they came out into the bush: low, grey, industrial suburbs, hills

257

and plains of single-storied houses jammed together, without a tree or a lawn or a flower. The only reds and greens and blues were on advertisements as gleaming, provocative and numerous as the jewels of Aladdin's cave. Such white and yellow, black and gold! Such lines and curves of colour! They were the gardens, the sights, of the suburbs. Children learned to read from them: through them they were introduced to art.

They drove through streets of closed and bolted shops where large cats slept among the softening fruit in greengrocers' windows, and flies walked miles across the pink-icing pastures of Saturday's unsold cakes. Bicycle shops and shoe shops, hotels and cinemas.

It was deserted as no-man's land so early on a Sunday morning: an occasional, monumental, newspaper vendor stood on a corner, his papers and placards grouped round him. Stray children flew zig-zag like swallows across the empty streets.

At last the suburbs rushed away and the shape of the land could be seen again: semi-bushland scattered with farms, vineyards and orchards. Stalls offering eggs and tomatoes and flowers for sale joggled one another at crossroads, and cows grazed in the paddocks. They neared the looming wall of mountains and began the ascent.

The wireless played all the time. Interspersed with advertisements for shaving cream and lawnmowers, on record after record, American voices proclaimed the invincibility of love, love, love. It's the only thing, they said.

Stan joined the crooners. Once, when he heard the lyric properly, he snorted with incredulous amusement. 'Did you hear that? The poor coot's goin' mad!'

Esther smiled faintly. 'It's understandable.'

And that really made him laugh.

When they reached Katoomba, on the Blue Mountains, it was disappointingly hot and dusty, covered by Sunday's peculiar pall. Aimless crowds stared and ambled, ate ice-cream and oranges, hung over the railings at Echo Point and cooed their breath away over the vast valley.

'Isn't it big? Isn't it blue? Wouldn't it be a long way to fall if I pushed you?'

But finding after a time that the valley was too deep, and the mountains too intensely blue, unteasable, not funny, most people wandered to cosier spots where humans could perform against human-sized backgrounds.

'Dunno,' said Stan doubtfully as they sat in the parked car on the rim of Jamieson Valley. 'Dunno if we shouldn't have gone somewhere else.' He looked at her.

'No, I'm glad we came here. It was worth coming just to look over the valley again. It's breathtaking, isn't it?'

'The Grand Canyon'll be bigger,' he grinned.

The day passed in a slow, hot haze. They drove round to some of the other beauty spots—waterfalls without water at this time of year, precipices complete with legends—and finally had lunch at a hotel.

The heat seemed to increase. Their faces grew flushed. Their clothes stuck to the leather of the seats and Stan cursed because he had forgotten to collect the covers on Saturday.

But in spite of all they smiled, talked, and Stan, at least, was happy. He was profoundly relieved to feel that he was starting again with the past clean, the future unmarred, and Esther was wrapped in confidence caught from his mood.

CHAPTER TWENTY-FOUR

A barmaid might want to make extra money. Wait. How did Laura know she was a barmaid? Cassie. She must have asked her friend. At least ten women do assembling work for Stan. She must be one of them. It's quite simple. Yes. But if she is? Why have I come? She will want to know. Stan will want to know. He would have to hear the whole story. He would call it checking-up. It would be much worse than accusing him. Then what?

Stan had left home at eight-thirty and Esther had waited until nine o'clock. Now as she crossed the busy intersection it was nearing twenty past nine. She had walked slowly, allowing herself to be jostled and passed by. But soon she would be there and she had nothing prepared as an excuse, no reason to offer the woman, or Stan. Her thoughts had not gone so far ahead. The necessity for a reason became apparent only now—now when she was almost there, when it seemed equally impossible to go back or forward.

I'd be surprised to find her at home at all at this time, she thought, and the feeling that she was persecuting some innocent hard-working woman increased with every step. Her intentions seemed, this morning, melodramatic, incredible, deceitful, and she wondered how it was, when she had so little desire, that she was borne so inexorably forward. There was a nightmarish quality in the steady clip-clip of her high heels, the sense of being powerless to change the decision taken in a moment of hysteria.

As she turned the corner of Baker Street to reach the main entrance to the towering red-brick building, Stan ran down the steps to the car. Like a slow-motion film, when she turned to the window of a shop, the scene ran again and again. He had been hurrying. She saw the movement of his arms and legs, the familiar bulge of junk in his pocket. She stood very still until at last she heard the sound of the engine starting up and the car moved off down the street, going straight ahead without turning to pass close to her. It disappeared round a corner some hundred yards ahead.

Stan said that he had some deliveries to make first thing this morning: he was bringing her materials. Was he? It's late. It took him a long time. What makes you think he came here first? He had several calls to make.

On a wall of the bare, marbled entrance hall the tenants' names and flat numbers were listed on white cards under glass. Mrs V. Rogers in Number Four. And Mrs Rogers must be in if Stan has just been here…If? You saw him. You said yourself he had deliveries to make. You see how it is. It's all right. Don't go up.

And she said, 'Four,' and climbed the stairs until she reached a dark door marked with a small figure four. She pressed the bell and waited. Almost at once she heard someone moving in the hall, hurrying, and then the door opened wide.

'Well? What did you forget?' Vi cried, holding Stan's cigarette case in the air. 'Oh!' She dropped her hand when she saw Esther. 'I though it was someone else—a friend. He's always forgetting things.'

'I'm Esther Peterson—Stan Peterson's wife. May I come in?'

Their eyes locked for a moment in silence, then Vi said, 'Yes, come in.'

Esther walked into the hall and Vi shut the door. She led the way. 'I don't go out to work till two on Mondays so I like to have a sleep-in while I've got the chance,' she said, thrusting her hands into the pockets of her silky-cotton housecoat, holding the skirt out in front of her.

As they crossed to the armchairs under the corner windows both women bent their heads at the blaze of sunshine that poured into the room.

'I am early,' Esther said. 'But Stan was even earlier, wasn't he? That was his case you had?' Her voice was calm.

Their eyes were inseparable, willed together. While the voices went slowly, haphazardly, to the point, they found immediate contact at the level of the heart.

Vi leaned back in her chair and took a deep breath. 'Yes, it's his,' she said dully, pulling it from her pocket and tossing it on the table. 'He had a message for me to pass on to one of the boys…Did you see him just now?'

'Yes.'

'He see you?'

'No.'

'Oh.'

There was a slight pause. Esther balked at the next question, paralysed by nausea. Finally she said, 'You don't work for Stan, do you, Mrs Rogers? You aren't connected with his business?'

With a look of smouldering anger Vi said, 'No I don't and no I'm not.'

'I see.'

Vi looked at her hands, mentally reviled herself for being shaken, hated her unsteady breathing and tried to restrain it, but added attention increased the quivering search for air. Her nerves strained. 'Why have you come? What's it all about? I think you'd better tell me.'

'I want to know—what is your connection with my husband?'

'Do you?' Vi said pleasantly. 'Your husband.' She stopped and bit her teeth together, looked at the windows. Esther gazed at her face, at her mouth and hair. Turning back, Vi asked, 'How did you know that there was a connection at all?'

'He was seen here.'

'Ah, yes, I suppose he would be...some kind friend...' The response was distracted, stock, as if she were not concerned in the affair. Her whole attention was bent inwards in an effort to control her increasing desire to shout the truth straight out, to tell her all she wanted to know and a lot more besides. She simply said, 'The connection is that I've known Stan for nearly twenty years. We're friends.'

'Are you...?'

'What else do you expect?'

'I don't quite know. What should I expect? You are an old friend, you say, of Stan's.'

'That's right.'

'That's not all, is it?'

'No, no, it's not,' Vi said with sick intensity, and the words revealed to both the cold abyss of an uncertain future to which they were now, by those words, irrevocably committed.

'For how long?'

'Oh, what's it matter? For years, a lot of years.' Vi slumped back and covered her eyes with her hands in a gesture of weariness. There was no exultation in her attitude. After a minute she said, 'Well, what happens now?'

Esther said, 'And after we were married?'

Some subtle change of expression, blind, stricken, on the face of the woman opposite her, communicated itself to Vi through some sense other than her eyes. Reluctantly she said, 'What's the matter? You're not going to faint or anything are you?'

'After we were married?'

Having expected abuse, tears, even violence, Esther's tight control weakened Vi. It made her tell the truth, called forth in her a certain answering restraint. It became in such an atmosphere as necessary for her to tell as for Esther to hear.

She said, 'I didn't see him for months.'

In the lack of response there was something that made Vi's head come up. 'If it's any satisfaction to you,' she said contemptuously. 'Oh, he tried all right. He's a boy wonder—Stan. Maybe he was having another little try just lately. He was away for just on seven weeks if you're interested. He's back, so I don't care if you know it. And I'll tell you that while he was playing Prince Charming to you, I didn't exist. He dropped me without a message, without a word!' She clenched her fists and leaned forward. 'But he came back, you see, and he's come back again, and I *took* him back, and I'll keep him as long as I can—make up your mind about that! We're old pals, Stan and me; I know him and he needs me whether he knows it or not. You didn't make him happy.'

Again, a silent warning, an intimation of some shrill sensation like an aching nerve, penetrated Vi's excited fluency and made her end a speech which, having begun to stir the old unvoiced bitterness of Stan's desertion, might have continued for hours without relieving her of all the pent-up jealousy and pain. 'Well, anyway...' she said heavily, eyeing Stan's wife.

At length Esther said, 'I thought you were married?'

'Was. He was killed in an accident two years afterwards. He was just a kid—twenty-two. I was twenty.'

Esther's eyes followed her as she took a cigarette from Stan's case, dropped the matches, stooped to pick them up, lit the cigarette and held it in a hand that shook.

'Stan could have married you at any time, then?'

Vi blew a cloud of smoke and waited. 'You've thought of that? He never did. He didn't care to, my dear.' She relapsed into her normal voice. 'He had bigger ideas.'

Then, as if to disavow her last remark, to cancel it out, she lay back with her eyes closed, her hand rising and falling now and then with the cigarette.

The details of the room in which they sat imposed themselves on Esther's eyes: the polished wooden floor, the pale rug, the green-and-white curtains. There was a photograph of a plump woman in old-fashioned dress beside the midget wireless set.

At the other end of the short hall she could see the pale blue bedroom, the unmade bed. She looked back at the closed face of the woman, the smooth round arms, the soft curves under the blue gown: talcum powder streaked one bare foot whose high-heeled mule had fallen off and lay sideways on the edge of the rug.

She stood up and walked to the window. She was again assailed by the quivering coldness of unrealised shock and loss. Vi opened her eyes.

To them both the room was a cage, and they were dangerous to each other; even so, to be imprisoned thus was to be safe from time and its consequences. An instinctive recognition of this kept them silent a moment longer. And then a small flame of anger, feebly inappropriate, made Esther say: 'It never occurred to you to send him away when he came back? You didn't, I suppose, think that that might be the thing to do?'

Vi stared at her in amazement. 'Oh, act your age! He came after *me*, remember? God knows I wanted him back, but he came to suit himself, because he wanted me. No one made him, and, no, I'm afraid I didn't think of sending him back to you.' After an almost exasperated pause, she said, 'Where did you live before you met him? In a convent?' She looked at her curiously. 'This is nothing new—this kind of thing—it happens all the time.'

While she had been speaking, Vi found her slipper and stood up. Standing in the middle of the floor they stared at one another as if in eyes and flesh there might be found a key.

Just then there came a banging at the front door, and a woman's hoarse voice, adding to the clamour, cried, 'It's me, dear.'

'Cleaner,' Vi said, and going to the door she called, 'Later, Daph, later.'

'Righto!'

The noise ceased and she came back, drawing the cord of her gown more tightly around her waist. 'I know you think so,' she said, 'but you haven't got it all your own way, you know, not by a long shot.'

'Perhaps not.' Her eyes on her clasped hands, Esther spoke almost patiently. 'In any case,' she said, 'it's all over now—this meeting,' she added, seeing Vi about to break forth again.

With slow steps and pauses they started to walk to the door. In what seemed a momentary enlargement of comprehension Esther experienced a frightening sense of human frailty and vulnerability. They were all in the power of something stronger than themselves, and to be pitied. But she could feel no pity, nothing.

'Well,' said Vi on a deep breath, 'now you've seen the low-life that's left by the tide. The girl from the pub and the kept woman in person. But not very much kept,' she added, putting her hand on the lock to open it. 'Don't kid yourself I'm in this for the profit.'

The door was open, but, knowing that there was

nothing to be done, they hesitated to say goodbye. The lack of precedent caused them at this late moment to regard each other with something of apology and resignation. The long pause, the expectation of a miracle, the waiting for the dream to break, and then the door closed and it was over.

In the street outside the day was lustrous with spring; spring-like and enchanting in the middle of summer. All the late humidity had cleared and the air was as light and clear as the shining sky.

Underfoot, brick, asphalt and stone were warm and dry. Today no dust blew through the crevices of the roads that covered the old land beneath.

CHAPTER TWENTY-FIVE

After ringing five numbers Vi finally heard Stan's voice coming through the receiver. 'What d'you want?' he asked peevishly. 'I'm busy.'

'Well, busy or not, come round as soon as you can. Come right away, Stan, it's important.'

Her urgency pierced through to him. 'Oh? What's up?'

She could see his eyes narrow, suddenly alert. 'I'll tell you when you get here. Don't be long.'

Just as she finished dressing he let himself in and came to the bedroom where he leaned against the door jamb, his hat pushed back, one leg crossed in front of the other.

'Well,' he said, 'what's it all about? What's the mystery?' He was protected from surprise by disdain, preoccupation.

'Come out here,' she said, and he followed her, swinging his car keys on the end of their silver chain.

He flopped into a chair and, without wasting any time, Vi told him what had happened.

He was impassive. 'Oh?...So she was here, was she?...Mmm.' He stretched his legs, smiled, and said, 'Mmm,' again on a note of such false interest that Vi became impatient.

'Yes, she was, for I don't know how long. We had quite a chat,' she said drily. '"What's your connection with my husband? You aren't just friends, are you?"...Friends!'

He lifted his brows. 'I'll bet you took damn good care to tell her, didn't you?'

'Oh, for Pete's sake! She only knows what she knew. No one had to spell it to her.'

Stan held her gaze solemnly, grimaced and looked away. 'This is lovely! Lovely!' he said, jumping up and walking about the room. He was still incredulous, but as belief began to grow, angry excitement, too, began to penetrate his defence.

'It isn't my fault,' Vi said. 'It was no fun for me.' On a lower note she added, 'Whatever happens, it isn't going to do me any good, I know that.'

'Yeah, yeah!' Stan shut her up with an impatient wave of his hand.

She dropped her forehead on her arm, and straightway he turned on her viciously. 'Don't let's have any waterworks!'

'What do you mean?' She lifted her head and he turned away without answering.

He went to the window and stood drumming his fingers on the sill. 'How was she?'

Vi put a hand to her throat as if to find some comfort in the touch of skin against skin.

'How *was* she?' As he repeated his question he strode across the room and stood glaring down at her as if he could scarcely restrain himself from violence.

She looked at him steadily, looked away. Dragging herself to her feet she said, 'How *would* she be? Try to guess. And how am *I*, if it comes to that? Thanks for your interest…not so hot.' There was a pause and she put a hand on his arm. 'Well, anyway, I'll leave you to it, I'm—'

'Why? Where are you going?' The anger was gone. He didn't want to be alone to think, to wonder what to do.

'Just through there,' she said, 'not to work, thank God, not till two.'

He let her go and wandered morosely back to his station at the window.

Trailing about her room, lifting a stocking from one chair, dropping it on another, Vi wondered stonily what would happen. The possibility that she might find herself the loser brought a pain that carried its own antidote.

The jealous strength conjured up by Esther's presence had been replaced by passivity. If it happens, it

273

does, she thought. I can't help it. And if she felt that her mood was an attempt at self-deception, she let the feeling lie in darkness.

A pearly breeze blew through the open window, played over her face, made her drop her hands and stand quiet.

'Can I come in now, Vi?' The banging at the door and the voice came simultaneously.

Starting a little she moved a step or two nearer to call back, 'Oh, no, Daph. Leave it for today, love.'

Then she heard Stan crashing through to her. 'What was that?'

'Cleaner—Daph.'

She put some shoes in the cupboard and began to tidy the bed. Stan watched her all the time with an air of brooding frustration and at last said, 'Well, I'm off!'

'Where to?

'Anywhere they've got some whisky.'

Vi stiffened. She went over to him. 'I wouldn't do that today, honey.'

'Wouldn't you? You know how interested I am in anything *you'd* do, don't you?' He leaned against the wall, his mouth curling with sarcasm.

'Okay. Okay!' she shrugged. 'It's your own business, I guess. But just…' She hesitated and he prompted, still eyeing her superciliously, 'But just?'

'Watch what you're doing—that's all.' He made no reply and she said after a moment, looking up at him, 'When'll I see you?'

'Soon,' he said, and pulled her into his arms. He gave her a hard, unloving kiss and let her go.

'No wonder I love you,' she said, pushing her hair back from her forehead. 'You're so...' She gave up and he laughed and said, 'Maybe I'll see you tonight or tomorrow.'

Stan drove out past Rose Bay to Watsons Bay, a quiet wealthy suburb set on the cliffs of the south head of the harbour. He went there for no particular reason except that it had seemed to him the quickest way to leave the city centre. The wide street, the white cement footpaths, were deserted. Parking the car, he climbed under the painted railing that separated the road from the tramlines, and, turning east, away from the houses and streets and harbour, crossed the few yards of rocky ground to a lookout platform that faced the ocean.

Hundreds of feet below, the Pacific slapped against the rocks at the base of the headland, and spread out in a tremendous arc, dark blue and calm, stretching away to the Americas. Stan wondered if he might not be looking in the direction of the South Pole.

Some freighters, coastal freighters, passed on the horizon which was today clear, a distinct line where the pale and the dark blue met. Behind him a tram rattled past beginning the journey into town, and the conductor, idle in the empty compartments, stared at the ocean as if it were magnetic. He noticed the solitary figure on the platform and envied him that he could stand there on such a morning.

The driver of the tram turned his head slightly as the conductor came up behind him and peered over his shoulder at the silver rails ahead.

'Bonzer day!' he said in an effort to express his appreciation of the radiance of air and sea.

'Sure is. Like a dip, wouldn't you?'

The shining rails curved away from the sea: the tram reached a stop, and a man and four women climbed in.

The piping at the top of the high fence was warm under his fingers. Stan gripped it tightly, then let it go. Ever since he had left Vi's apartment he had kept his mind clear of thought by some mental effort akin to the physical one of holding the breath. But now as the blood flowed again to the suddenly slack fingers, so the implications of Esther's discovery came to his brain, and he was alarmed.

If only someone would listen to *his* side of the story. But who would, except Esther or Vi, and what could he say to them that wouldn't send them into hysterics? Women and fuss, women and fuss! Well, to be fair, there was a lot to be said for them. But everything was going to be kind of awkward now for a while. Somehow, someone wasn't going to be pleased. He had a horrible feeling about that.

Gazing at the ground, he kicked a pebble through the wire-mesh fence. It doesn't look too good, he thought, and yet, is it so bad? Why should it matter so much to Est? Vi doesn't care about *her*.

He moved uneasily at the sound of his 'why' and his 'yet'. Of course it wasn't sensible but it *would* matter.

Falling into a mood of sentimental melancholy, he pictured himself as he had been before he met Esther, a garish picture of ignorance personified, and beside that he placed the latest model of Stan Peterson—not perfect, far from it, but a man of the world—a man who could make his way round confidently. And whose doing? Who—you might say—practically lived for him? Est, again, not Vi—Vi would always get along.

Est was different—expecting a fellow to be different, too, believing that he was, and because of that, making him feel lower than he was. Oh God, it was complicated. He scratched his head and expelled a sigh. That was the trouble. She honoured him—*she him*—in some outlandish way, in spite of everything, rows and drinks and everything.

'Oh hell!' he said aloud, and screwed up his eyes, noticing again where he was. He could still see the freighters, but they had moved well apart by this time.

How in hell's name did she find out anyway? he wondered, enveloped in contrariness all at once, as usual feeling aggrieved with fate for doing this to him. He went so far as to convince himself that curiosity

277

discovered what it deserved, but his dishonesty nagged at him until he let the swollen bag of self-justification deflate.

So it'll be the worst thing that's ever happened. It'll be the end of the world. He knew it, and he did not like it. The thought of facing her was quite a thought.

He took out a cigarette and as he did a voice behind him said: 'Got a light?'

A young man of nineteen or twenty, thin and dark-haired, stood grinning at him. His eyes were blue, his clothes cheap and flashy. 'Got a cigarette?' he said when Stan held out his lighter. He took one from the packet with the sinister deliberation of an American film gang-ster. 'Thanks, mate,' he said cheerily. They stood side by side for a minute, not talking. Stan wished that the boy would disappear as he had come. When, instead, he pointed to the extreme edge of the cliff and said, 'Hear about the joker that jumped over the other night?' Stan turned to go. 'No,' he said repressively and went back under the railing to the car.

'So long, mate,' the voice called after him, faintly ironic.

He moved out from the kerb and drove back to town. At first he drove fast, glad to be urged by indigna-tion against the intrusion on his lonely platform, pleased to have even so flimsy a thought to occupy his attention.

But as he neared the city he slowed down, trying dismally to decide where to go, what to do. In spite of his declaration he didn't want to go to a pub. But what was the alternative? Back to Eddie's where he had been when Vi phoned? He crawled along. No business, he thought, not yet awhile. And not Est, certainly not back home. That only leaves Vi.

As the thought formed his energy rose again and his face lightened. He could do something positive—constructive. What he had said about tonight or tomorrow wasn't true. Mightn't come off at all, ever.

He knew himself well enough to realise that he would very likely promise Est that he wouldn't see Vi again. And if he did, he vowed, if it was really necessary, he would stick to his word. But this time he would tell her it was over.

It was true that Vi had claims on him—not for money, of course, only for her company, really—but still, if it had to end, whose fault was it? Hang it all, he was *married* to Est. She had to come first even if it was tough on Vi.

His mind veered from side to side, stopped and started as easily as the car responded to the fingertip control of the wheel. It was time to be reasonable, Stan decided, and he allowed every variation of his mind and will to come under the scope of the term.

When he reached Vi's rooms she was out, and he wondered with a touch of apprehension if he shouldn't take this as a sign and disappear before she returned. Seeing Est later on was going to be bad enough without acting the hero and coming back to make a farewell speech.

Hands in pockets, head bent, he scuffed from room to room, his mind turning on Esther, on Esther exclusively. When he believed that she would not come, he heard a key in the door, and a moment later Vi was in the room holding a brown paper shopping bag, looking at him blankly.

'Stan!' she said, not putting the bag down, staring at him as if she would read his thoughts.

He noticed now, though he had not earlier in the morning, that she was wearing a dress he had not seen before.

'Well,' she said, letting the bag drop to the table, 'what's happened?'

'Nothing. I just came back. Nothing else to do.'

Though her mind was almost paralysed with worry, she smiled, for this was not bad news, and said distractedly, 'Oh, is that all.' She heaved her groceries a stage further, to the kitchen. 'When are you going to go...?'

'God knows.' He ambled over to the door and looked at her as she distributed her purchases around the various cupboards and bins.

Sunlight exploded from every piece of nickel and chrome in the room. It fell refracted on walls and ceiling and floor. Vi's face was creamy in it, her arms pale apricot.

Stan stared and stared at her, gloomily, not seeing her in the present, but looking back from the future and reliving this moment in memory. His eyes dulled. What a nostalgic value she assumed when he looked at her, perhaps for the last time!

'I'll have to go soon.' She was wretchedly aware that the time during which she might ask questions, exact promises, was passing. After all my threats, she thought, and though everything depends on it, I just sit dumb and wait for things to happen.

Forcing herself to look at Stan with something of her old assurance, she said, 'Have you thought…Do you know what happens to us? To me?…This won't make any difference to us, will it?' She gave him a smile but he kept his eyes on the ground.

With a sudden frenzied premonition of grief she put her hands on his face and turned his eyes towards her own.

'Oh God!' she cried when she had gazed at him for a second. 'Was this you coming back to say, "Cheerio, Vi. I have to go home and be a good boy now"?'

Aggrieved to find himself so easily read he did not reply, and she said, 'That was it, wasn't it…?' A moment's thought made her ask, 'What if she won't have you back?'

'Don't you worry about that,' he said smoothly, convincing her—for how could she know how they were together?—at some cost to his own confidence.

At his tone, and her belief, Vi was diminished. 'Oh, come on, honey, we haven't got time for a row. But

281

you're not going to tell me it's all over, are you? We're too used to each other. I don't know what's right and what's wrong about it, Stan; lately none of it's been good. I only know we've been together too long for it to happen like this—haven't we?' She brought her face close to his for her eyes seemed strangely blind.

'Sure, sure. That's right,' said Stan. 'We won't lose touch.'

'Oh…I see…We won't lose touch.' She said it very slowly, deliberately, to give herself time to think again after those words had reached her brain and heart. 'So that's why you haven't seen her yet—why you haven't talked to her. You've decided to get me off your conscience first so that you can tell her it's all over. That's the way it is, isn't it?'

'Well, what if it is?' he said, crossing his legs. 'You have to be sensible about these things. You and me, we've had our good days. You've been a great pal, you were my whole family, for years, I *know* it. But…'

'You'd better remember to put that in your reference.'

'And I was the same for you. All right. But I've given Est a pretty rough time and I think it's about time she had a fair deal. As long as she didn't know, well, there was no harm done…'

Vi exclaimed in disgust, 'How funny can you get? Don't try to make me laugh because I can tell you, I don't feel like it.'

'You'll be all right,' he persisted. 'You don't want

to stick to a character like me all your days. You ought to settle down. You won't be short of offers.'

After a protracted silence Vi said in a dull, flat voice, 'Well, well…You're a gentle little boy, aren't you? A real nice kid! Still,' she roused herself somehow and moved, 'that's not news. You haven't changed, I'll say that for you. Still the same boy I always knew.' She had been holding her hands tightly together, now she half laughed and put a hand to her cheek.

Her resistance seeming to have ceased, Stan was abruptly halted. It was time for him to go if he meant to go—if he did not, this course was no longer safe. Vi's resignation might procure in him a perversity of will, a switch of motive, that neither tears nor recriminations could have achieved.

On an impulse he lied to her, retaining to himself wordlessly, in a distant country of his mind, the right to decide in the vague future, when events were clear, his exact intention.

He said, 'It's not the way you see it, Vi. I need Est. I have to keep in with her. Why do you think I married her?'

She was quite still, suspended and pulseless, unhopeful, knowing that he wanted her to say, 'Why did you?'

'She's got money,' he said uneasily and their eyes came together, held, parted.

Vi dared not breathe until she believed. 'Oh God,

283

is that true? Was that it? Is it true, Stan...? For heaven's sake, look at me and tell me.'

The reluctance with which he repeated the statement began to persuade where protestations would have failed. She knew that he was proud, above all else, of his ability to make money—that it showed him to be, after all, not self-sufficient must make this admission doubly shameful to him.

She said, 'What about me...? I've got some money. You could have told me.'

'I said *money*.'

'So you did...Then what was all that just now about being sensible and so on? What were you trying to do?'

He stood up impatiently. 'Oh, use your head!...Got anything to drink?'

'In the fridge.'

He came back with two glasses of beer and handed one to her. 'Look, I've told you. I've got to keep in with her. I thought, now she knows, maybe I'd have to stay away a while: I thought maybe it'd be better if I didn't tell you about all this, if we broke it up so you'd have a chance to get out and maybe—oh, I don't know what I thought. The whole bloody business is enough to drive anyone round the bend, isn't it, kid?'

Vi took this in while he drank his beer. She looked from him to the glass he had given her and held it up. He took it willingly.

'You changed your mind,' she said.

Stan wiped his mouth with the back of his hand. He drew a mock-solemn face. 'Looks like it.'

There could be heard a laugh of shock and relief which seemed not to have come from the woman who, unsmiling, rose to wander a few steps across the room.

'Whatever you meant to do,' she turned to say, 'you did it too damned well. It was a rotten thing to do to me, Stan. Don't ever try anything like that again—just don't!' She fell back on the sofa and flapped her hands in front of her face. 'God, I feel as limp as a jellyfish. I'm dead...And *you*!'

Looking at him, without warning she began to cry hopelessly, not knowing why, but knowing there was reason. 'After all those months away—you didn't have to stay so long—and you never told me why—it wasn't fair—and never coming near me all that time...'

'Sure, sure. It was lousy.' Stan tried to take her hands. Disregarded, he walked away, but presently said, 'How about a drink now?'

She nodded. 'Tea.'

'Go and fix yourself up and I'll get some, then.'

Shortly afterwards they sat talking: Stan was saying, 'Remember that time I came into your dad's place in Brisbane? That was a day wasn't it?...Remember that shindy when old Salty Marshall...'

'Went and told Eck...?' Vi laughed.

'Yeah,' Stan chuckled.

285

'What made you think about that?'

'Dunno.'

'Bet I've got some snaps we took up there. I'll have a look for them tonight.'

With a flash of excitement Stan said, 'I don't remember seeing them. Wonder how old we were then? What do you think? Twenty-one?'

'About that—must have been.'

Stan lifted her fingers one at a time, testing each one to see how far back it would bend. He had fallen into an abstracted silence and was living over some old adventure when all at once, remembering, he groaned and stretched his arms above his head.

And Vi, who had not forgotten, said, 'Yes.'

He grimaced and rubbed a hand over his face. 'Well...I suppose I'd better go.' Then in answer to her unspoken question he said, 'I'll have to see how I get on—oh God, I should get back to Eddie, too—well, I'll ring, or come in tomorrow for sure. If I have to keep away from here for a while we'll see what we can do. Maybe you should move—I don't know. Anyhow!' He kissed her, and then, slightly loosening his hold, their faces just a few inches apart, breathing each other's familiar breath, they stared in a kind of heavy calm. After what seemed a great tract of time, Stan said stolidly, 'Well, this is it!' At Vi's instant change, he added, 'I just meant—I'd better be off.'

'Oh! Yes.' She began, 'You'd better...' and stopped.

She was unsure how she had meant to go on. Almost anything, at this point, could be wrong.

Watching him go, she was assailed by feelings of a complexity she did not care to probe.

CHAPTER TWENTY-SIX

Bob Demster hailed her from the open doorway of his flat. 'Tell Stan I've fixed up a game for him and Bill Maitland for next Saturday, will you?'

'Yes,' she said, not smiling, not turning her head, and he looked after her, surprised and disgruntled.

An uneven circular route had brought her home through miles of busy, sun-swept streets: perhaps one hour had passed. Now like a visitor she sat in the armchair that was never used, and gazed with an occasional flicker of her lashes at what lay in front of her. It was the table, still covered with breakfast dishes. She could see that the butter had begun to melt. After a time, with a movement, stiff, somehow burdened, she rose and shifted the dish six inches into a spar of shade cast by the window frame, and, having done that, went onto the balcony. It was hot there. She felt the heat strike her body and the heat rise in her to meet it. The rough edge of the brick wall penetrated the soft pads of her fingers as she leaned, for a moment, forward. An inclination to rest her cheek against the warm brick was halted by the sight of two women passing below.

Inside again, she returned to the chair which seemed by virtue of its lack of associations the only place in the room where she might with safety rest.

When, much later, from the wireless in a neighbouring flat, an announcement of the time was understood by her, she crossed to the table and, stacking plate on plate, collected crusts of toast in a hand that seemed uncertain what to do with them. Some seconds passed while she eyed them with dismay—hard crusts of toast—their disposal so grievous a problem that her fortitude might fail before it could be solved. The slow realisation that a postponement of decision was, after all, possible, brought with it a sensation of relief that made her lean against the sink for support. She dropped the scraps in a heap on the draining board, and the telephone in the bedroom rang. With cold curiosity she listened to the screech-screech of its bell, held more by the sound than what it signified, until at length it stopped.

And then she thought: It could have been him.

By no moisture of eye, or trembling of hands, by no frown did she betray the blankness of her spirit, the exhaustion of her heart. That she was she, that this was her one life, her past and future, she most tiredly knew.

The dishes done and put away, in the middle of the small kitchen, Esther slowly smoothed her narrow dress. A sound at the door suspended her thus, head bent, palms flat against her thighs, the warm movement of skin on silk never to be completed.

Straightening, as he could be heard in the hall, she gave a sigh, and turned on the empty room, into which he was about to come, a look that changed at last to one of calm. Going forward to meet him, she said, 'Hello, Stan.'

Text Classics